# Boy Band Blues

# Kelly McKain

USBORNE

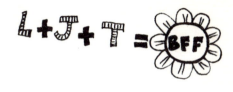

# My
# <u>totally secret</u>
# journal

## by

## Lucy Jessica Hartley

<u>Dun! Dun-dun-dun!</u>
<u>This is the 6 o'clock news</u>
<u>on Thursday the 3rd of March.</u>
BONG-G-G! BONG-G-G! BONG-G-G!
BONG-G-G! BONG-G-G! BONG-G-G!

This is meant to be like the Big Ben bonging
thing they have at the start of the news
on telly, BTW. (BTW is text language for
By The Way, By The Way.)

Good Evening. This is Lucy Jessica Hartley
returning from Not Writing Land to bring you a
very important newsflash. Since winning the

Fantasy Fashion Competition (for full juicy details
check out my last journal, which is actually *called*
Fantasy Fashion), something very exciting has
happened. Lucy Jessica Hartley, the Year 8 schoolgirl,
loving daughter, not-so-loving sister (well, little
bros can be a nightmare!) and general fashion
goddess has been asked to style a boy band!

The news broke early this morning, after
assembly, when Lucy was approached in the corridor
by Wayne Roman, the guitar-toting lust-object of the
upper school. Unlike most of the girls at Tambridge
High, Lucy doesn't fancy Wayne Roman at all. Okay,
he is good-looking but he is also a total big-head, and
anyway it's good-lookingness in that really obvious
film-star way which Lucy finds massively yawn-
making. So, after Lucy had stopped nearly dying of
amazement that a Year 10 would approach a Year 8 in
broad daylight, a short conversation ensued (I think
that's the right word but I'm not sure).

The full details of this meeting cannot be
disclosed for security reasons, however we can

release the following statement: "We at the LJH press office are pleased to announce that, following her success in the Fantasy Fashion Comp (and after getting congratulated in assembly), Lucy has agreed to take on the role of band stylist and general image coordinator, or style coordinator, or maybe image consultant. Lucy is in fact still deciding on the coolest name for the job."

So, how brilliant is that!?! Mum reckons when someone asks you to do something specified like styling a band because of your skills it is called a commission. I myself in fact think it is called the *Hand of Fate* smiling down at me. I have been feeling the *Hand of Fate* in my life recently because of winning the Fantasy Fashion Comp and because of Dad staying here in Sherborne doing his radio station job instead of going around the world for about 2 years being a roadie.

Okay, as an update of my life, here is a list of things I am waiting for at the moment.

# Lucy Jessica Hartley's Waiting List

1. I am still waiting for Dad to come back and fix my new door handle the right way round so it goes down instead of up. Dad does not actually live here any more because he and Mum split up in September, and he CRUELLY ABANDONED us to go and live at Uncle Ken's. When Mum saw the upwards-going handle she folded her arms and said that Dad meant well, but that his DIY skills were "far from exceptional". That was quite polite for her because they normally just do bickering down the phone.

   Anyway, the reason I needed a new door handle is because this weird thing happened. Basically, me and Alex (my little bro – nuff said) were standing in my doorway having a sensible and mature discussion about whether or not he should be allowed into my room, and

8

it just fell off for no reason. Okay, maybe we were yanking it a tiny bit, but it's just that my **BFF** Jules and Tilda *(BFF means Best Friends Forever, BTW, which is what me and Tilda and Jules are.)* were round and we were discussing the very important and secret topic of Qs. *(Will explain later.)*

2. I am also still waiting for my mum to lend me her new **MAC** eyeshadow, which is this gorgeous shimmery grey colour that absolutely perfectly matches my eyes. Of course, when I am a real, actual fashion designer, which is my lifetime's ambition, I will get loads of **MAC** stuff free, but till then I have to borrow it from Mum. I tried to cadge a bit of the eyeshadow yesterday by doing flattery, which means saying, "Oh, Mum, you are so beautiful and gorgeous already that you don't need make-up. Why don't you lend that eyeshadow to me instead?" I knew it was working because she did this happy laugh so I said a bit more to seal the deal, which was,

"And of course, Dad's gone now and you never have any time or money to go out with your friends so it's not like anyone sees it anyway." Weirdly enough, she still wouldn't let me borrow it, even though she said, "Thanks, Lu, you make me feel so good about myself," and instantly treated herself to a chocolate éclair.

3. I am in fact also still waiting for my Q... Oh, look, I can tell you about it here, so you didn't have to wait very long in actual fact. Q means period (the boys in my class are mainly immature idiots, so we made up a code word in case they overhear us talking about it at school, and P was too obvious so we changed it to Q). Tilda got hers at the end of October, but I will probably be about 24 when I get mine. I don't know why I'm bothering to even start waiting yet, because I am a *late developer*, as this tape-measure woman in Marks and Sparks's bra department called it. At least Jules hasn't started yet either, so her and Tilda have

not reached matureness together without me. I have recently tried predicting when my Q will arrive with the pendulum from my Teen Witch Kit that Tilda and Jules got me for winning the Fantasy Fashion Comp. The pendulum said my Q would come last week, and I got all excited and kept going to the toilet to check, but nothing happened, apart from Mum asking me if I'd eaten a dodgy prawn. So I don't know if the pendulum is broken, or if it made a wrong prediction because in my subconsciousness I moved my hand to give it a bit of help in the "yes" direction.

So, anyway, I was saying about the boy band commission thing. Our school is hosting a Battle of the Bands Competition for all the local schools in aid of charity. Wayne wants to put a band together and win the competition for the highly artistic reason (NOT) that "the St. Cecilia's girls are coming and they are HOT, man!"

Styling a band is basically the same as on *Pop Idol* where you get this rambly bunch together and then after the shopping and the hair styling and stuff they look like a proper band. I think it will be more of a band made out of boys than an actual boy band, though. This is because actual boy bands involve synchronized dancing, which I don't reckon Wayne Roman would be keen on doing (although he is a *whizz* on the rugby pitch).

Also, the rest of the band is made out of Jack Stone and Joe Black who are famous for bunking

Jack Stone

Wayne Roman

Joe Black

off games lessons, so any actual exercise might instantly kill them. It's lucky that Wayne Roman is being the lead singer and not Jack or Joe because they don't tend to speak in normal words, but more in just grunts. And someone grunting to music is not going to make a hit single in my opinion.

Anyway, we are having our first proper meeting tomorrow at breaktime. I am bringing Tilda and Jules as my assistants and they have already started being mega-helpful. For example, Jules has offered to measure Wayne Roman's inside leg, and Tilda says she will take his jeans home to customize them. They are both so sweet to give up their time to help me, even though they are not that into fashion designing.

Hey, I just thought, wouldn't it be cool if there was a magic image-changing machine? Like, called the style-O-Matic 500 or something. You could just walk in as your normal self and then come out the other side with a new look, like this:

I am kind of like the *Style-O-Matic 500*
except I take a bit longer. Also, sometimes I have
to persuade people to have a makeover but with a
machine you could just shove them in. In fact,
Tilda used to be Matilda-Jane who thought fashion
was a woolly jumper with a horse head knitted on
the front till I did a total re-style on her. She
wasn't sure about her new look at first, but she
loves it now!

Tilda has been my other **BFF** since then, so now we go round as a three with Jules. Tilda is in actual fact half Hollandish (hang on, I mean Dutch) and she lives with only her dad, 'cos her mum died when she was really little. She just told us that fact, but she never said exactly what happened, and she never talks about it, so we don't say anything. I tried to mention it one or two times at first but I didn't really know what to say, and Tilda quickly changed the subject.

My other **BFF** Jules is actually called Julietta Garcia Perez Benedicionatorio. She has been my **BFF** since primary school when we got put together for a three-legged race at Sports Day and we won because of our cooperational skills. Jules is all Spanishly fiery and passionate so sometimes we fall out, but hopefully you will not have to read about that in this journal because we are very-nearly-teenagers and we are getting extremely mature. Soon we will not fall out ever but just go for coffee and that instead. Jules also has an older brother called JJ who is **très** lush. When I used to have a big crush on him, he said he didn't *not* like me, so that was cool. But he is still going out with Suzanna with the big you-know-whats so it's lucky I'm completely over him.

Well, I have to go and have tea now, which is in fact shepherd's pie (wonder why it's called that?!). I promise, promise, promise that I'll write in here after the band meeting tomorrow, but it probably won't be straight after school because I have to go and see Dad at his new job in the radio station. I can't wait – it's going to be *soooooo* cool!

*Byeeeeee!*

# Friday

I am writing this in the loos at lunchtime because Tilda is at her piano lesson and Jules is at drama club and Simon Driscott is at computer club with the Geeky Minions so I'm all on my own. (BTW Simon Driscott is this boy in my class who I used to call the Prince of Pillockdom because he has a strange lopsided haircut and thinks that Star Trek is way cool. The Geeky Minions trail round after him like clones. There was an Embarrassing Incident at the school disco in November which I will not go into - *shiver* - but since then I have found out that he is an okay boy and we are sort of like friends now.)

Well, I quickly had to write this now to tell you about the first band meeting and also about something else which is a complete secret – shhh! It is in fact a secret about Tilda but it is such a *secret* secret that me and Jules haven't actually even told Tilda herself that we have found out. Okay, so what happened was this...

We were meeting Tilda and the band at the old music room at first break, which is in the Victorian part of the school and which is *mega-ly* creepy. Year 11 sometimes use it for drama, but it's mainly empty since they created the new music centre. I don't get why they bothered doing that because people playing glockenspiels badly is the same in one room as in another really, isn't it? Anyway, Mr. Phillips said the boys could use the old music room for band practice but only till it starts getting turned into an IT centre next month. Why are they always turning everything into a centre, BTW? Are they trying to fool us that it is not in actual fact still *school?!*

Me and Jules were walking up on our own because Tilda was coming straight from the brainy maths set, which us two are definitely not in. When we opened the door, you know the piano behind the felt board thing? Oh, right, you don't 'cos of not going to my school, but anyway there is one and we heard it PLAYING!

# GULP!

The music was this plinkety-plonk Victorian stuff so I instantly thought there was a ghost behind the board. I gripped Jules's arm and whispered to her that we most likely had a *supernatural emergency* on our hands.

Jules frowned at me and went, "I don't think ghosts really play the piano, Lu."

"*shhh!* They do if they are a poltergeist," I whispered. That made us both completely scared because poltergeists are those ones that can make your head spin round and green projectile vomit come flying out of you, although *that* would just blend in nicely with our gross-o-matic uniforms.

Then this completely beautiful singing started up with the music. It was the sort of song that young ladies used to sing after dinner before telly was invented, going on about the bounteous meadow and the soaring lark and that. That's when I decided it was definitely a Victorian lady poltergeist, because no modern alive person would decide to sing a song like that when there is Kylie instead.

We went closer to the board, creeping up, while I was desperately trying to remember what my Teen Witch Kit said about poltergeists.

Then I suddenly remembered that it said poltergeists are far too dangerous to be dealt with by even the most proficient Teen Witch and that they should be left to the professionals.

## DOUBLE GULP!

Anyway, it was too late to get professionals so we stuck our trembling heads round the board and *phew* it was not a ghost, but TILDA! We knew she went to piano, of course, because she does it about 2 lunchtimes a week, but we had no idea she could sing like that. I mean, it was really, really good, like, strong and powerful, even if it was a really, really awful song. In choir her singing is all timid and wavery, and it suddenly veers off onto wrong notes without warning, like my dad changing lanes on the motorway. I just couldn't understand why she wouldn't tell us she is secretly amazing. I suppose it is because she's so shy in front of people that her voice doesn't come out very well normally. Also, she doesn't like to blow her own trumpet (weird phrase, but at least it's to do with music!).

Jules was about to start clapping, both with commendation to Tilda and relief about the poltergeist, but knowing how shy Tilda is I just grabbed Jules by the arm and pulled her away. We crept right back to the door and I said, "Don't tell Tilda we saw her 'cos she'll get totally embarrassed." Jules agreed, luckily, and so then we opened the door really loud and came in again, chatting and that. Tilda instantly stopped singing and came out from behind the board.

After about 10 minutes, when we were just about to give up waiting for the band and go back to the loos, where we usually hang around at break, they turned up. They had probably been held up by Wayne Roman having to fight his way through a crowd of adoring girls or something — I really don't get that, personally.

Joe and Jack grunted in a sorry kind of way, but Wayne Roman didn't even apologize or anything. Sadly, Jules and Tilda were too busy staring at him mushily to even notice so it was up to me to say, "Don't apologize or anything."

He grinned at me in this annoying way and went, "Yeah, right, like Year 8s have got anything better to do at break."

Charming! He makes me so... Grr...

"Anyway," I said, "have you got a name for the band yet?" That is called Moving Swiftly On and is the professional thing to do when you have to work with someone annoying.

"I thought we could just be called Wayne Roman," said you've-guessed-who (see what I mean about vain!). Luckily Joe and Jack grunted their unhappiness about that.

"Well, how about something simple, say just a

letter," Wayne suggested then, looking a bit grumpy. "Like Q."

Of course, me and the girls instantly started laughing, because then they would be in a band called a codeword for *period*.

Wayne Roman rolled his eyes at us like we were little kids giggling babyishly, which Tilda and Jules noticed so they just went back to staring adoringly. Wayne Roman *soooooo* thinks he is *God's Gift to Girls*, which is stupid because everyone knows *God's Gift to Girls* is actually glitter nail tattoos.

"Well, if that's so funny, why don't you come up with something better?" Wayne Roman went, all moodyishly.

Even though I am a creative person, it was horrible to just be asked straight out like that, and have everyone staring at me. Still, I had to quickly think of something and the only thing that was still in my mind that wasn't to do with *periods* was *names*, so I said, "How about Blackstone?"

Joe Black and Jack Stone both grunted "cool". Wayne Roman looked even moodier but he didn't suggest anything else so he'd obviously already used up the 2 brain cells rattling round in his head. Tilda and Jules liked Blackstone muchly of course, because they are

WAYNE'S BRAIN

ONLY 2 BRAIN CELLS!

my loyal **BFF**, and so it was decided.

We arranged to meet up at Tuesday break to hear the band rehearse so I could get the image right and that. Sorry to mention this again, but Wayne Roman is SERIOUSLY annoying. I don't get why he is so offish with me when he asked me to style the band in the first place. And I don't know why he thinks he's above us just 'cos he's in Year 10. Everyone knows girls are at least 2 years more mature than boys anyway.

Hey, maybe I will design his trousers so that

they fall down onstage! That will serve him right. Plus, I will tell him it's cool to wear *ginormous* boxers like my dad does and then when the trousers come off everyone will see his really bad pant sense and laugh.

## Friday night,

lying on my bed eating a
Tracker. I have seen Dad
at work, but I have not seen Wayne
Roman since this morning, luckily!!!!

After school today I dropped in on Dad at work
to tell him about the boy band commission thing.
2 weeks ago he started at **WICKED FM**, our local
radio station. Before I went there I had
this idea of him being really surprised
and delighted to see me and me
being led up to his office and
getting a coffee out of those
machine things where
everything is numbered
so, like, people just say
"I'll have a 31, please",
and your drink comes out
magically free. Then I

imagined that I would sit on the
swivel chair for visitors and Dad
would sit at a desk in front of me with gold
records on the wall behind him, and buzz his
secretary to *Hold The Phone* because his
daughter had arrived. I don't know why I thought
that because it was in fact *not* the reality. When I
got there I found no coffee machine, and instead
Dad was actually *making* the coffee. He looked
really surprised to see me but not exactly
delighted. He was going, "Hello, love, erm, what
are you doing here?" and I said, "Washing my
socks," to be funny, but he didn't get that. "Seeing
you, of course," I said instead, and then I added,

"and mine's black with 2 sugars."

He did laugh then like I was being funny, but in fact I was being serious. I have decided to start drinking coffee because it's really grown-up and they are always doing it in *Friends*. Plus then you can say to people, "Hey, shall we go for a coffee?" which sounds *soooooo* cool.

So, normally, Dad looks all laid-back because he is in Uncle Ken's flat strumming his guitar and watching his pants dry. Since he left his job as the manager of our local Sainsbury's the only time he gets steamed up is having a row on the phone with Mum. But today he looked all stressed out, and then he said, "It's nice to see you, Lu, but I've got a million things to do, I can't really stop."

I said, "That's okay, I'll just wait in your office and sit in your swivel chair for visitors."

Dad blinked at me. "Office?" he repeated. "Yeah, *right*! Lucy, I've got a tiny desk in the corner of reception, but I spend most of the day just running around."

28

I went, "Oh."

Then this girl who looked about 20, with spiky pink hair, stuck her head out of one of the studios. I instantly hated her, even before she said, "Hey, Bri, my man! Any chance of that coffee this millennium? I know you can't move fast with that zimmer frame, but…"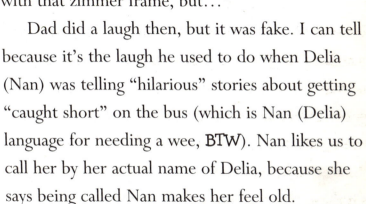

Dad did a laugh then, but it was fake. I can tell because it's the laugh he used to do when Delia (Nan) was telling "hilarious" stories about getting "caught short" on the bus (which is Nan (Delia) language for needing a wee, **BTW**). Nan likes us to call her by her actual name of Delia, because she says being called Nan makes her feel old.

I just wanted Miss Spiky Pink Head to drop instantly dead, like **THUD**! But she didn't so I blurted out something like, "Yeah, well, my dad might be twice as old as you are but he's still totally rock and roll. And it's not like he's *old* old, as in having embarrassing nasal hair!"

I said that because Dad is not over 50, and I once saw an advert for this, like, mini combine-harvester thing men stick up their noses, that looks like this:

Torture-O-Matic 800

The advert said "Over 50? Embarrassing nasal hair? Rip it out with the Torture-O-Matic 800!" or something like that

The girl looked at me and went, "You're *sooo* funny!"

*Grrrr!* Why do people always say that when I am totally **NOT** meaning to be! Then Dad handed her the coffee and she went "Ta" and vanished again. Dad said, "Age is weird. I look like an old wrinkly, but inside I still feel like I'm 18." Huh, I wonder if I will reach 18 and then feel like it for ever, or if that is just Dad.

"Don't worry, you'll get on the radio," I went.

Dad just sighed. "I don't think so, Lu. You've seen how young Sally is, and the other DJs are all like that too. I think my only chance to be on air is if I ring in to request a song!"

I was just trying to think of something else helpful to say when Dad suddenly jumped up and went to hand out the coffees. After that I fidgeted around while he franked some parcels for the post, which is this machine way of doing it instead of using stamps. Then at last he had 5 minutes so I told him about the boy-band thing. I thought he might be excited like Mum was, or sound interested at least, but he just got really grumpy and went, "Well, good luck to them if they want to throw their lives away on an impossible dream. Rock and roll is a hard master, Lu. It takes no prisoners." (I was thinking, *eh?*, by this point, not getting him at all.) "It messes you up if you're successful and it messes you up if you're not," he went then. "You're damned if you do and you're damned if you don't." (By then I was like, *double eh?*)

"Great, right, okay, thanks, that really helps," I said, all confused. I grabbed my bag and headed off then. Why would Dad be so totally weird? He's got his new job in the music industry and, okay, maybe not the swivel chair for visitors, but that will probably come when he gets promoted. Plus, he's still near to me and Alex, which is what he wanted, and he even seems to be getting on better with Mum. Everything should be okay now, shouldn't it?

Well, that's what I thought at that exact moment anyway...but then I had a rethink because of the stuff I am about to write.

What happened was, when I got in just now I had a hot chocolate with Mum and told her about how the band thing went and about how annoying Wayne Roman is.

Mum went, "Lucy, I know this is a wonderful thing to be asked to do, and I'm really behind you, but I'm not sure about you hanging around with Year 10 boys."

I went, "Mum, don't worry. Even though all the other girls on Planet Earth think Wayne Roman is totally lush, actually he's a repulsive big-head, and

32

Joe and Jack don't even talk, but just do grunting. So, there's no way I would want to snog any of them!"

(I have in actual fact snogged someone, who is called Dog Boy, but I'm not telling Mum about that. Dog Boy was my boyfriend for about 2 weeks after the Fantasy Fashion Competition, but I chucked him. He was really nice but he wanted to spend, like, ALL his time with me, when I wanted to see my friends and work on my fashion ideas and stuff.)

Mum then snorted into her hot chocolate and her cheeks went bright red. "Lucy!" she cried. "I didn't quite… Er, I was actually thinking about the effect on your schoolwork… But now you've put that idea in my head as well!" She put her mug down and sighed. "Oh, dear, I suppose I'll have to get used to all this now you're nearly 13."

My brain did some fast thinking then. "Maybe if you could meet them you'd feel happier," I said.

"They could come round on Saturday so that me and Tilda and Jules can sort out their T-shirts and jeans and that. Only to make you feel better, of course."

Mum was quiet for a minute and then she got up and went, "Oh, wonderful, a house full of teenagers on my lovely quiet weekend."

So I took that as a yes. I got up too and got a fork to start nicking bits out of the casserole thing on the stove. Mum slapped my hand away, saying, "Ah, ah, don't you go eating the best bits out of it as usual!"

Why do parents always say "as usual" when things have only happened once?! **BTW**, Mum is only talking about this **ONE** time when I was about 8 and she had this dinner party. She went to dish up a rustic Italian sausage cassoulet and there were no bits of rustic Italian sausage left in it, only juice and these beans that were like baked beans but with the sauce washed off.

"Anyway, that's not for us, it's for your father," Mum said.

*What?!* The casserole smelled really good, so I said, "But he only likes curries! I think *we* should have this."

Mum sighed. "Oh, Lu, he's got no money for takeaways at the moment, and I thought some home cooking would cheer him up."

"Well, he does need cheering up," I admitted. "He was so grumpy today when I asked him about the boy band. He said with a career in rock and roll you're damned if you do and you're damned if you don't."

"What lovely language," said Mum sarkily, reaching into the fridge for a chocolate éclair. "Lu, I think maybe he feels he's missed his own chance to be famous, and he's finding it hard to accept that he's not going to be in the music industry."

"But he *is* in it," I said. "He's working at WICKED FM."

"Well, I don't know if that's going anywhere,

unfortunately. There's an opening coming up at the station for a DJ but Robert Hyde, his boss, won't let him audition for it, because he doesn't have any experience. It's a shame because he's been practising really hard in the flat. He gave me a demo, and I have to admit he's actually quite good."

That made me feel angry and upset at the same time, like I wanted to march in there and make Dad's boss give him a go. "I bet it's 'cos he's older than that stupid Miss Spiky Pink Head," I grumped. "But you *have* to give old people a chance, don't you? It's the law!"

Mum sighed. "Lu, between you and me I think it *is* to do with age, yes. But Robert also has a legitimate reason in your father's lack of experience, so there's not a lot we can do."

Then *Neighbours* came on, so we sort of stopped talking about it. But now I have written this down and read it back I have had the **REVELATION** that Mum is right about Dad still being unfulfilled and that.

Oh double triple bumheads! It is *my* fault Dad is unfulfilled, 'cos he was going away to follow his dream by being a roadie but I threw this brilliant Rock Party for him. It made him get how much he'd miss us and that's what made him decide to stay and work at the radio station. And now he is miserable. But how can I change things? The roadie job will be gone by now, and anyway I still don't want him to leave Sherborne. And if he can't try out for the DJ job either… Oh, I *soooooo* wish there was something I could do to change his boss's mind. I will have a hard think about it because maybe there is.

In fact, I will start right now by watching *Friends* on DVD, which always helps me come up with ways to solve difficult problems. I've explained that to Mum, but she still won't let me do my maths homework in front of it, for some reason.

## Tuesday

I still don't like Wayne Roman, BTW.

So we heard the band play today, and it was surprisingly okay. Me and Jules and Tilda were the audience. It was just these 2 covers of The Libertines and The White Stripes, and I was right about there being no synchronized dancing. The fact that Joe Black and Jack Stone act really bored when they are playing actually looks quite cool. Luckily I was looking at all of them and writing notes and ideas about their image, because Jules and Tilda were mainly just staring at Wayne Roman. He was singing really flirtily to us, and he kept lowering his head so his silly blond hair flopped in his face. I bet he was imagining standing in front of a load of screaming St. Cecilia's girls.

Anyway, I am controlling myself from writing any more because I have to get on with my ideas. Right now. So I'm going. So I'll stop writing. So *byeeeeee!*

# Wednesday

Good and bad.

Good because I did not have to see Wayne Roman AT ALL – yay!

Bad because I saw this lasagne in the fridge this morning and I was looking forward to it all day, and then when I got home it was in fact no longer there. When I interrogated Mum later she said she'd made it for Dad and taken it round there, and she told me they had a cup of coffee and an actual chat as well, without shouting, just about. The just about bit was because some of the chat was Dad asking her if she'd put on weight, but she said she did the "counting to 5 before saying anything" exercise that she got out of her book called *Raising Teenagers – The Most Rewarding Years*. Then she said after the counting she had an *Empowering Moment* and realized she doesn't care what Dad thinks any

39

more, so she didn't bother with the shouting.

Well, good for her and everything, but when I made them promise to get on better, I didn't mean that she should give him the best dinner so we only end up with fish fingers, beans and chips. I did notice that Mum only had a few chips though, and no ice cream for dessert with me and Alex. Huh! Maybe she does care what Dad thinks after all.

# Thursday

I am soooooo making those trick falling-off trousers for Wayne Roman.

**W**e went to the old music room today at break to show the boys some ideas I have had, which are:

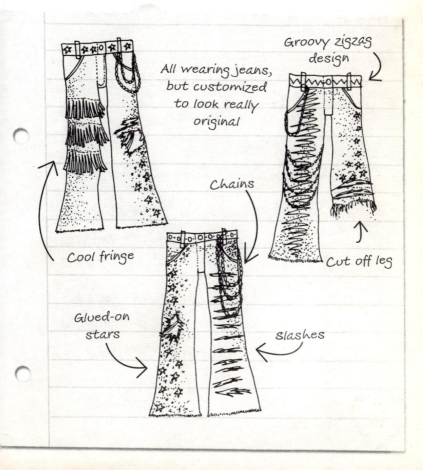

Groovy zigzag design

All wearing jeans, but customized to look really original

Chains

Cool fringe

Cut off leg

Glued-on stars

Slashes

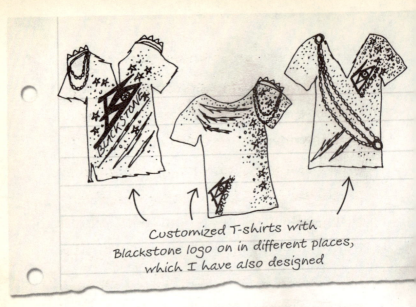

Customized T-shirts with
Blackstone logo on in different places,
which I have also designed

When I was waiting for them to actually turn
up I also did this list.

☆ The Main Reasons Why I ☆
Hate
Do ~~Not Like~~ Wayne Roman

1. When he speaks to me he is always so snidey
   and sneery it makes me go bright red with
   anger.

2. Then when I do think of what to say back, the
   way he stares at me with his annoyingly big
   blue eyes (which are sort of the colour of a

Mediterranean sea at sunset) puts me off.

3. Then, because I am a professional, I stop myself saying what I was going to say by clamping my teeth together really hard. This looks like I'm grinning madly at him, so he probably thinks I fancy him or something – yuckorama!

4. To do my job I have to keep looking at the photo I took of him with Tilda's camera – I even had to stick it on my pin board, which unfortunately means I can see it from nearly everywhere in my room. I am also doing sketches of ideas for his hairstyle and clothes and that – so I am CONSTANTLY having to think of him, which reminds me how much I hate him.

I have got lots of the bits and pieces for customizing their jeans and 3 plain black T-shirts to transform with my T-shirt printing set, so I am all ready now.

_Friday_

I should be happy it's
the weekend but unluckily
I have to see Wayne Roman
again tomorrow. Boo! Hiss!

**W**ow, the most amazingly weird thing happened round Jules's after school. Me and Tilda were there watching _Buffy_ DVDs as usual, and Buffy and Spike were beating each other up, also as usual.

I said to my two **BFF**, "Now that is what I would like to do to Wayne Roman because I hate, hate and triple hate him!"

Then this absolutely awful thing happened.

Buffy and Spike stopped fighting and started snogging.

**Eeeeeek!**

So next I was staring at the TV with my eyes goggling out, going, "What are they possibly _doing_?"

Jules pretended she had to squint right up to the TV and went all sarky, going, "Erm, I'm not sure. It looks like they might be kissing, but we'll have to wait for the results to come back from the lab."

I swiped at her, yelling, "But they hate each other! Buffy hates Spike as much as I hate Wayne Roman! I even wrote a list of things I hate about him!"

Jules swiped me back, going, "Don't worry, Lu, this is TV, not real life."

"Unless…" said Tilda, very quietly.

"What?" I went, whirling around.

I must have snapped a bit 'cos Tilda looked hurt and fiddled with one of her long blonde plaits. "Nothing," she mumbled.

"Oh, come on, Tilda," I said, all softly-softly, "we are all three BFF. There's nothing you can't tell me."

Tilda looked highly doubtful and went, "I think I can't tell you *this*."

But I have this Natural Curiosity that means I absolutely have to know things, so I kept saying,

"Come on, come on, *pur-leeeeeeeeease*
tell me."

Jules really wanted to know too, so she got
some bacon crisps out of the kitchen, which are
Tilda's favourite because she's not
allowed them at home (her dad is
quite stricty about what food
she eats). She dangled them in
front of Tilda's face and went,
*"Pur-leasy-please-please."*

"I am not saying this for bacon crisps but for
Lucy's own benefit," Tilda said, although she
grabbed the packet anyway. Then she said to me,
"Have you got that list of things you hate about
Wayne Roman *(chomp chomp)*?"

I dug this journal out of my bag and read out
the list. Tilda listened a lot and Jules only listened
a bit because she was mainly still watching
Buffy.

"What if you look at the list differently?"
said Tilda.

"You mean like turn it upside down?" I asked, feeling confused.

"Kind of," said Tilda. "I mean, when you see Wayne Roman you go red and tongue-tied, and you grin madly at him. Maybe instead of hating him you actually have a massive crush on him." She blurted this out really quickly and then ducked behind a cushion, expecting me to go crazy on her.

But I was too busy being in **SHOCKED STUNNEDNESS**. So was Jules because *Buffy* had just ended and she was properly listening. I told Tilda she is *soooooo* wrong. There is no way on the Planet Earth I would have a crush on Wayne Roman, not ever ever ever. Excuse me, but I am still in such **SHOCKED STUNNEDNESS** about Tilda saying such an impossible thing that I have to go and lie down in a darkened room.

# Saturday night

Tilda and Jules have just gone home, and I have been left with a messy room to clear up, melted wax on my carpet and about one billion things to tell you.

NEWSFLASH! Tilda is *soooooo* right! I have a massive crush on Wayne Roman! Shock and amazement, you are thinking!!! I am thinking that too. But I know it is true because I tested it by using science. (I used to be rubbish at science, but since I did my homework report on Operation Makeover Matilda-Jane, instead of that thing with the Bunsen burner we did in class, I have been Mrs. Stepton's favourite.)

In science you first of all get a theory and then you check it by finding evidence. Okay, so this is what happened today when the band came round:

*Tilda's Theory:* That I have a massive crush on Wayne Roman.

*Evidence:* Well, first of all, the band came round my house, looking all shambolical. Wayne Roman was wearing black jeans and a blue hooded top that brought out the deep blue flecks in his eyes. "Afternoon, Mrs. Hartley," he went all politely. Joe Black and Jack Stone were grunting as usual. So *Evidence 1* is that I noticed what Wayne Roman wore, and also I was so busy staring at his speckly eyes that I forgot to hold my breath and nearly died of the smell when Joe Black and Jack Stone took their trainers off at the door.

We got some drinks and that and went upstairs, where Tilda and Jules were waiting. The boys handed over their bags, which had their band jeans in, and I had to show Wayne how I was going to customize his for when he was onstage. I was going, "I'll make slashes here and here," and kind of drawing it in the air with my finger.

Jules went, "Show Wayne properly on the

trousers that he is actually wearing, Lucy." Jules was just testing the evidence about me fancying Wayne by making me have to actually touch him. So I had to run my *actual* finger along his *actual* leg, which made me want to jump out of the window with a giant attack of *cringitis*, and so that is *Evidence 2*.

*Evidence 3* is that I nearly died when he said my CD collection was cool. In fact, he was not looking at *my* CD collection, but a rack of Dad's that he is meant to come and pick up. They are only even *in* my room because I was looking at the covers for logo ideas for Blackstone. But obviously I wasn't going to mention that. Wayne said how some of those songs and artists are way cool, and I impressed him by telling him about all the secret meanings in that "American Pie" song – like how the lyrics are really about Buddy Holly and the Beatles and Bob Dylan and that. Wayne looked completely impressed. At last, listening to Dad droning on about it has come in useful!

Then Wayne said could he put on "Free Fallin'" because he loved it, and I said totally yes because I love it too (which I honestly do – it's the one that me and Jules always sing, and Tilda likes it as well even though she never joins in). Joe and Jack also liked it, and so they all decided that it would be the actual song they do at the concert. I was *mega-ly* excited about Wayne singing one of my fave songs, but then he spoiled it by asking how on earth I could know about Tom Petty and the Heartbreakers when I am just a tiny infant. Well, maybe he didn't quite say that but his tone of voice had "kid" written all over it. Oh, it is terrible to fancy someone who doesn't fancy you back, though hopefully it will not be for long if my spell works. *(This is a secret thing but I will tell you about it later – shhhh!)*

"My dad's into this kind of music actually, so I grew up liking cool stuff," I said, a bit annoyedly.

"In fact Dad plays the guitar *and* he works at the radio station."

"Cool," said Joe Black.

"DJs rock," said Jack Stone.

Which, BTW, also proves scientifically that they do know how to communicate in the language of English and not just by grunting.

And at that exact same moment Wayne Roman looked at me in a 100% impressed way. "Wow, how cool that your dad's a DJ," he went.

"Yeah," I said. It wasn't lying exactly. I mean, I didn't start the thing off that Dad is a DJ, Jack did. I meant to tell Wayne the truth, about Dad being the running-around man instead, but weirdly my lips got sort of paralysed while I was staring into his eyes that are like pools of crystal azure water.

Luckily Jules and Tilda were downstairs slashing Joe's band jeans with Mum's new Kitchen Devils knife at that exact time, or they would have said, hang on a minute, your dad is not an actual

DJ. When they came back upstairs I got them quickly into doing the T-shirt printing, so that no one would start talking about Dad again.

Evidence 4 is that I obviously care what Wayne thinks of me because as soon as I realized about Evidence 1, 2, and 3 I desperately started trying to hide my soft toys and other embarrassingly stupid baby stuff, including my Barbies. Obviously I know that they are for trying out designs in mini form first so I can see if they work without spending a lot on material. But Wayne Roman does NOT know that. Probably he thinks I've got them for playing with! Most cringe-making was that I have a Ken who I had done a little outfit on of how I was going to customize Wayne's clothes for the concert. I was just trying to throw it out of the window when Wayne turned around and went, "Oh, look, you've done your Ken up like me."

I don't even have to TELL you how embarrassing that was. I don't know what embarrassment is measured in, but if it was pounds it would be about £5,000,000,000

and if it was in Richters like an earthquake it would be however many is off the scale and if it was in per cent it would be 155%, which is not factually possible, but that is how embarrassing it was.

Luckily then the boys went home, and Jules made cheese sandwiches for us, and Mum said we could take them up to my room. I told Jules and Tilda my scientific discovery that I did in fact fancy Wayne Roman. Jules squealed, but Tilda just looked all spiritually wise like she knew it all along. Jules is happy because now we are a three in fancying Wayne Roman, whereas before it was just those two (plus all the other girls in the school actually, but she is only bothered about our group).

After that I had done so much science that I was in danger of turning into a Geeky Minion so I decided to tackle this fancying problem by using witchcraft instead. So we looked in my Teen Witch Kit to see what it said under Boys. There was this warning thing saying that you shouldn't try to use witchcraft to influence a boy into liking you, because that is *enchantment*, which goes against free will. Luckily on the next page there was a spell to make your own self irresistible, and then it's up to the boy to like you out of his own free will, so that's okay.

So I wanted to do the spell and Jules and Tilda were really keen as well because then we will all be irresistible and it will be up to Wayne to choose who he likes (oh, please let it be *meeeeeee!*).

So anyway, the spell was:

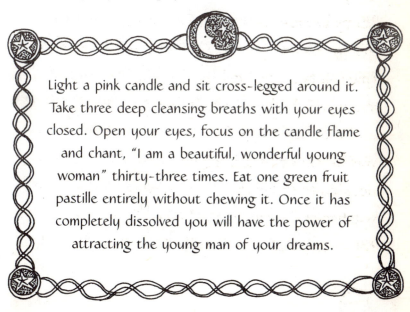

Light a pink candle and sit cross-legged around it. Take three deep cleansing breaths with your eyes closed. Open your eyes, focus on the candle flame and chant, "I am a beautiful, wonderful young woman" thirty-three times. Eat one green fruit pastille entirely without chewing it. Once it has completely dissolved you will have the power of attracting the young man of your dreams.

Well, for a start I liked the bit about being a young woman and not a girl — that is because of it being a kit for teenagers, which we very nearly are. We had a bit of trouble finding a pink candle — there was only a very small little bit left of the elephant-shaped scented one Gloria gave Mum for having relaxing baths to unwind from the stress. (I don't know from the stress of what, but…) So anyway, we used that, but we had to chant pretty fast before it burned away.

Jules started off acting stupid in the chant, by doing it all sarkily, but then I said, "Do you want me and Tilda to have the magic power of attracting Wayne Roman without you?" and after that she was sensible. Tilda whispered the chant very very quietly as she was really embarrassed about calling herself beautiful, because she doesn't think she is. (*Soooooo* NOT true 'cos she is!)

The green fruit pastille bit was hardest, though, firstly because Jules had to lure Alex out of his room by asking him to show her some karate in the living room, then secondly I had to sneak in there and find where he was hiding his giant tube of them from Christmas (how has he still got them in March when I ate all mine on Boxing Day?), and then thirdly the non-chewing.

We all kept showing our tongues with the fruit pastilles on to prove we were not chewing. We were concentrating so hard on the not chewing that the candle got down really low and that's how wax spilled on the carpet. Anyway, we are *mega-ly* excited about going to school on Monday to see if the spell has worked. I also have this secret plan to keep saying the chant all tomorrow as well just in case the magic is true, so then I will get even more. This is fair because I fancy Wayne Roman much, much more than they do so I should have more magic. I wish it was Monday now, so I could see him. I feel like I want to spend all my time with him. Oh, I've just had this **REVELATION** that this must be how Dog Boy felt about me when we were going out, and I didn't like it. Right then, I will remember that and try to play it a tiny bit cool in front of Wayne, i.e. not actually dribbling on him at least.

Huh! Alex has just come in here and said, "Please don't go in my room when you're not invited, and also you owe me 3 green fruit pastilles. By the way, what is your Ken doing on the kitchen roof?"

**Yeeeek!** What kind of freaky little brother is it who counts his fruit pastilles every day? Now you can see what I have to put up with in this house!

# Monday the 14th of March,

and I am now over the actual moon with joyfulness. It is last break, which is the very first chance I've had to write in here, I promise!!! I have even come straight to English 15 minutes early so I can sit in peace and quiet and write this, even though that has left Jules and Tilda in a two without me.

**W**ell, I have to tell you that I completely believe in my Teen Witch Kit after today!!! What happened was that science was straight after lunch and I stayed behind a bit after it because Mrs. Stepton was explaining this thing to me we did in class that I just entirely did not get, and when I came out Wayne Roman's group were lined up along the wall. Well, Wayne Roman himself was more *leaning* than lining, because lining up is *soooooo* uncool. I was **MORTIFIED** *(this means so embarrassed you could just drop actually dead, BTW)* because I wasn't prepared to see him. I tried to sneak past to get to the loos and make myself look better but he said, "Lucy, wait up! I was hoping to run into you. You're looking especially beautiful and wonderful today."

That's how I know the spell has worked because I was still wearing my disgusting green science overall that is the shape of a sack, and I had embarrassing safety goggle marks around my eyes, but he still said the exact words from the chant. *spooky or what?!*

"Yeah, so things are going well with the band," he went then.

"Yeah?" I went back, desperately trying to wiggle out of my overall while rubbing the red lines off my face at the same time.

"Yeah, we rehearsed in Joe's garage all of yesterday, and we're getting really good."

"Yeah?" I went again. It was all I could say

because my head was sort of half stuck in my overall because I'd tried to get it off quick without undoing any buttons.

"Yeah, so I was thinking, forget just entering the Battle of the Bands Competition, we could be, like, famous and stuff, man."

"Yeah?" I went, still stuck in my overall in total darkness with my oxygen slowly running out.

"Yeah. I mean, I just wanted to enter it to impress those hot St. Cecilia's girls, but now there's a girl I like *here* I'm not bothered about them any more."

Then I was thinking, oh wow, does he mean *here* at this school or *here* standing right in front of him, struggling to get out of her overall alive? Luckily, with my last few grams of strength I managed to get the stupid thing off my head. I was just in time to see his sizzling blue eyes looking straight at me in a very meaningful way. I am pretty sure he was talking about the girl right in front of him, *i.e. me!!*

"So, if you can think of any way we can get some airtime and stuff…" he said, giving me a totally eyeball-burning look.

"Yeah," I went, 'cos that was all I could think of, 'cos my brain was going into overdrive about how he hinted that he likes me.

"It's like you really get me, Luce," he went then. "You know just the right things to say."

"Yeah," I went again, because that is all I had said, and if he thought that made me totally get him then I wanted to keep saying it, obviously. Then he sort of leaned over me, and I thought he was going to say something else, but then Mrs. Stepton opened the door and they all started going in to science.

Isn't it annoying when you're in the middle of something really important and school gets in the way?

Wayne started walking, and I was in a sort of trance from looking into his eyes so I just started walking too, and before I knew it I was banging into Mrs. Stepton.

"How wonderful to see you again, Lucy!" she went. "You're obviously such a fan of my science classes that you've come back for more!"

Then this girl, Tamsin, who has a really gross foundation line round her neck, went, "It's not science she's a fan of, Miss," and all her Year 10 friends giggled.

I went bright red then, but luckily Wayne had already gone in so he didn't see. Mrs. Stepton chivvied them all in and said to everyone about getting their books out and opening them at page 23. Then she said really quietly to me, "Lucy, charming though he is, don't get any ideas about our Mr. Roman, will you?"

I did this fake laugh like, *Oh, what are you possibly talking about?* But I really wanted to say, *Actually, Miss, it is too late because if there are ideas to be got I have already got them.*

Mrs. Stepton sighed and said, "Off you go then, you'll be late for Geography."

Huh, I wonder why she said that thing about Wayne Roman? It must be because she doesn't think crushes should cross the barriers between the upper and lower school. Well, I don't care because no one can stand in our way. Not even Mrs. Stepton, not even wearing her very tough Scholl sandals.

This is because of a very secret reason, and I haven't even told Jules and Tilda yet, so no telling anyone, okay?

The fact is that I don't just have a crush on Wayne Roman.

The fact is, for the first time in my whole entire life I am in

And not just *Actual Love*, but *Forbidden Love*.

I know this because of Shakespeare — you know, that beardy play writer from the olden days when men wore tights and said "Forsooth, m'lady" all the time? Anyway, in English we are reading *Romeo and Juliet* by him, which is all about being in Forbidden Love with someone who no one thinks you should go out with.

## Signs of Being in Forbidden Love (which I have got from Romeo and Juliet)

1. Still wanting to go out with someone, even though your family doesn't approve. (Well, Mum did say I was too young to hang around with Year 10 boys, so that counts as her not approving. Juliet's cousin did try to beat Romeo up, though, which is a bit worse. But my only boy cousin is 4½ years old so I don't think Wayne's in danger.)

2. Getting other people to give messages for you, like Juliet got her nurse to, so you can

meet up with your secret love. Today I got
Jules to pass a note to Wayne Roman that
looked like this:

> Meet us in the old music
> room for a meeting at
> lunchtime.
> From,
> Lucy Jessica Hartley.

The spell must have only worked for me,
because Jules said nothing at all happened
when she passed him the note, and Tilda said
she got to the meeting first, and he was there
and he didn't say anything at all, and instead
was just checking his adorable floppy blond
hair in the mirror. (How nice that he cares
about how he looks when most boys are too
lazy to bother – how could I ever have thought
that was a bad thing?!) Anyway, when I got
there he didn't say anything specially to me,

so Tilda and Jules will hardly believe me about just now – but I will show them!

3. Juliet was actually 12 years old in the play, the same as me – *spooky or what?!* – but Mr. Wright doesn't mention that in English because there are some rudie bits where Romeo climbs in her bedroom window.

"Oh, Romeo, you're so manly!"

"Eeeeeek! I've snagged my tights!"

In those days if you weren't married by about 16 you were like an *Old Maid* but now it is modern times we get to *Enjoy Our Youth* and not be an *Old Maid* until massively,

massively old, like about 25 or something.

4. I have been sighing and going, "Wherefore art thou Wayne Roman?" all day like Juliet does about Romeo. I did stop when brainy Tilda said that actually meant *why* is he Wayne Roman not *where* is Wayne, because obviously I know *why* he is Wayne, don't I? ('Cos that's his name, *duh!*)

5. The last sign of being in *Forbidden Love* is a horrible violent death. But hopefully I will not have to do the drinking poison or the stabbing myself with a dagger that happens at the end of *Romeo and Juliet*.

So, apart from number 5, I am in *Forbidden Love* exactly like Romeo and Juliet were.

*Hee hee!* Mr. Wright just walked in and looked in complete shocked and stunnedness and went, "Lucy! You're reading Shakespeare! And taking notes!!"

As a joke I looked at the book like I didn't

know what it was and went, "Hang on, you mean this isn't *Vogue*?!" Then I said, "Even though Mr. William S. is a beardy bloke from the olden days when men wore actual tights there is still a lot in here to do with modern-day very-nearly-teenagers, you know."

Mr. Wright said that he had to go to the staffroom and have a cup of hot sweet tea for shock.

I said, "I know it's a surprise that a career girl like me can also be in *Forbidden Love*, like Juliet. But that is the fact."

Mr. Wright peered at me, looking like he found that funny. "Who's that with then?"

*Another person who thinks I'm being funny when I'm not! Grrr!*

I just did the zipping up my lips sign and went back to writing this.

Then Mr. Wright said that he should send me outside for my "Fresh Air and Exercise" as it was breaktime, but seeing as I would only go in the loos and experiment with eyeliner he was going to let me stay in and study.

First I was just amazed that he knew what eyeliner was, then I was suddenly struck by a good idea. Wow, it must be true that reading makes you more brainy! By staring at Mr. Wright, who is in charge of organizing the Battle of the Bands Competition, I realized how I could help the band get airtime and stuff, like Wayne wants. I also realized how I could get Dad on the radio as a DJ, even if it's just for 5 minutes on one night. Then it will be definitely true that he is a DJ, instead of not quite so true.

I said, "Actually, Mr. Wright, before you go and recover from my literariness, I know how we can get even more publicity for the Battle of the Bands." And then I told him my good idea.

I would tell you as well, but I have to go now because even though *Romeo and Juliet* is massively interesting, I do actually want to go and experiment with eyeliner in the loos, and plus tell Jules and Tilda that I am in *Forbidden Love*. I'll write more later. **Byeeeeee!**

## Tuesday night

after school when I am meant to be doing my homework - oops!

**W**ell, I can tell you that Mr. Wright totally loved my idea, and when I told Jules and Tilda about it they loved it too. This is a photocopy of the precise letter I dropped into the radio station last night, under the disguise of pretending to visit Dad.

Dear Sally,

Can I call you Sally?

Anyway, my name is Julietta Garcia Perez Benedicionatorio, and I am a pupil at Tambridge High.

I am writing to ask you a huge, massive favour

(Not my real name, obviously, but I don't want Sally to realize the surname and tell Dad it was me who invited her.)

71

as I am such a big fan of your show on Wicked FM.
Our school is hosting a Battle of the Bands
Competition on Saturday the 26th of
March starting at 5 p.m. There will be bands
there from all the local schools and we are joining
together as a community and stuff, even snooty
St. Cecilia's, so it is going to be really good for our
personal and social education. Plus it is a pound to
get in and all the money is going to the N.S.P.C.C.
so it's in a good cause. So I was wondering if you
could possibly maybe fit it into your schedule to
come along and cover it live for your listeners? Our
teacher, Mr. Wright, who is organizing it, says it
would be great if you could come as he is a big
fan too.
Yours in fingers-crossedness,
Julietta Garcia Perez Benedicionatorio
Tel: 07812 168

My mobile. Genius or what?

72

Of course I am not Sally Benson's huge fan — she is the horrible Miss Spiky Pink Head who said my dad needed a zimmer frame. But if she comes then I can do my plan to get Dad on the radio, which is:

 ## The Mad Fan Plan

1. Sally Benson comes to the concert.
2. Just when the band before Blackstone go on, she gets a phone  call (from me!) and quickly goes outside to take it.
3. While she is out there some mad fans mob her for autographs and that (I am going to ask Simon Driscott if I can borrow the Geeky Minions for this), and she can't get away, and she is late back.
4. Instead of having *Dead Air*, which is a really bad thing on the radio and means silence, Dad will step in and do the intro for Blackstone.

5. Robert Hyde will hear it and think how great Dad is and give him a job as a DJ!

It will only be for a few minutes on one night, but it will totally prove to Dad's boss that he is not too ancient to be a good DJ. The *Mad Fan Plan* is a little bit naughty so I haven't even told Tilda and Jules about it…

Oh hang on, maybe I shouldn't have even told you about it in case anyone extra opens this book and finds out. Extra people should beware that if they do read this, they will get cursed by the Teen Witch Kit as I have put a *Girls Only* spell on this journal. That especially means you, Alexander James Hartley – *if you read any more your eyes will pop right out of your head and dangle* – but not yet, it will only happen when you are 19. So you'd better stop reading unless you want a nasty surprise when you're at university or something!!!

Anyway, this secretary person for Sally Benson

74

called my mobile in English this morning and said that Sally would be *"delighted"* to come. (Why do adults always say they are *"delighted"* to do things?!) Mr. Wright was about to get cross about me having my moby on, but I told him it was the radio station about the Battle of the Bands and that they were coming. He just grumbled something about school rules being for the benefit of all, *young lady*, but he did look a little bit pleased.

The best thing of it all was when I happened to bump into Wayne Roman. Well, okay, in fact I was hiding round the corner until I spotted him coming out of his classroom. Anyway, when I told him about the radio station coming along and how Blackstone would get *some airtime and stuff* to help them get famous he picked me up in a hug!!!

Then he said, "Thank your dad for me, he's such a cool bloke!"

And I said, "Yeah," again, wishing the concert would hurry up so that my dad will then be an actual DJ and what Wayne thinks will be true and I won't feel bad any more.

Then that Gross Foundation Line girl, Tamsin, came out of the classroom and gave me the most dirty of looks, but I didn't care because – prepare to be amazed – Wayne was just at that second inviting me and the girls to a party Joe Black is having on Saturday night! Ha!

Well, I knew that my mum would never let me go in a zillion years. Plus I know that Jules's mum wouldn't let her either, 'cos our parents have a pact to stick together like glue. I didn't even *bother* wondering if Tilda would be allowed 'cos I know there is *No Way, José*. Her dad is v. v. stricty so it's not even in the stratosphere of *likely-ness*.

*(Another weird saying! I wonder who José is?)*

So I was about to make an ingenious excuse like already going clubbing in London, when Tamsin said, "Wayne, when Joe said you could invite people he didn't mean CHILDREN."

That was when I found myself suddenly saying "YES" for all three of us, straight away on the spot. Then I flounced off doing my catwalk swagger I learned from an actual proper model when I was at London Fashion Week with Stella Boyd. Eeeeeek! Now I have to actually GO to the party or look like a tiny infant in front of Wayne Roman, but how can I go there when I'll never be allowed?

Huh! Why is it that in LIFE you just sort out one tricky situation and you get another one?

And BTW, what is UP with that Tamsin girl? Why is she so horrible to me? Hey, I know, I bet she fancies Wayne and she doesn't like it that since last Saturday he has fancied me. I suppose I am going to have to put up with a lot of crazy jealousy from Year 10s when I am Wayne Roman's girlfriend. Still, it will be a million zillion times worth it.

## Wednesday night

Great day 'cos I saw Wayne
in the corridor and he went,
"All right?" and I went, "Yeah."
He is just so brill to talk to!

I just had to quickly write this before I get on
with finishing the jeans for the band, because look
what I found in my bag:

Dear Lucy,
Turn the radio on to
wicked F.M. at 8.10 A.M.

Wow or
what?!

I wonder who put that there? I hope it is who
I think it is!

Now I have to finish sewing the cool black
fringe down the side of Joe's jeans.

Oh, **BTW**, I told Jules about the party when we

walked home from school. We have decided that we are definitely both going, by hook or by actual shepherd's crook. I nearly rang up Tilda then, but I knew there was no point. Jules's idea was she wouldn't be allowed anyway so to be kind we should not tell her or invite her. But I think we should all be together for this historic event.

So, my idea is this:

### ☆ The Going For a Completely ☆ Usual Walk Plan

1. On Saturday we invite Tilda to mine for a video night and sleepover.
2. We ask Mum if we can go for a quick walk to get Jules's toothbrush that she forgot.
3. We drop into Joe's house just for one second to talk about the band.
4. We accidentally sort of end up at the party. **HA-HA-HAAAAAA!**

← Evil-genius laugh!

This way Tilda won't even know about the party, so she won't have the terrible bad choice of having to lie to her dad or stay at home (and I know Tilda would stay at home, so…). So me and Jules have decided we are doing my idea because we are all three **BFF**, and we should all go or it's not fair, especially since our **BFF**ness was made even stronger today by us going round with linked arms singing "Free Fallin'" (well, me and Jules were, and Tilda was miming). It was *sooooooo* funny when we came round a corner and crashed into Simon Driscott. We were giggling and he was going "Ow"! Then he said, "Why are you singing that?" and I said, "Just 'cos it's my favourite song and no other reason." And then we did more giggling 'cos really we were singing it to secretly show we fancy Wayne Roman. Simon Driscott did this look at me, meaning, *Girls are weird*, and then walked off, probably to computer club or in search of the Geeky Minions.

Anyway, I'm going on again. I really have to do Joe's jeans now and writing and sewing are not 2 things I can do at once, so *byeeeeee*!

# Thursday at 8.15 a.m.

**Eeeeeek!** The song on the radio just now was "Free Fallin'" by Tom Petty and the Heartbreakers, the one that Blackstone is doing for the concert!!! The DJ said it was to Lucy from her secret admirer. It must be from *Wayne*!!! I can't really show my excitement in words (but if you jump up and down waving your arms and going "*Yessity-yes-yes!!!!!!!!*" hopefully you'll get how I feel).

I *soooooo* want Wayne to ask me out. Or maybe I could ask *him* out, and save waiting. Now I definitely know he likes me, I *could* ask him, couldn't I? Modern girls *can* ask boys, in actual fact. I just looked in my Teen Witch Kit but the book doesn't tell you what to do when the boy you have attracted with the spell definitely likes you back.

Hang on…

Well, I just tried swinging the pendulum that

comes with the kit and it went the way I decided was for *Yes, definitely ask him out right now* and not the way for *No, don't ask him because you will make a complete idiot of yourself.* To be honest I only decided what way was which after it had started swinging, but it still counts. Doesn't it?

## Still Thursday

I am writing this in the loos
at first break because I just
came in here to get ready to do
a thing that I've decided to do...

Before I do the thing I just said about, I'll quickly
tell you that in English I did a survey of opinions
about "Can a girl ask a boy out?"

Tilda said no way because she would be too shy.

Jules said, "Yeah, course," but we know she is
also too shy deep down behind her cool chick-ness
because when she had a crush on Charlie P. she did
not ask him out one little bit.

Then I was busy because I knew all about the
Romeo and Juliet stuff we were discussing in the
class discussion, and so I kept putting my hand up
and making Mr. Wright completely amazed. But
then I accidentally said "Roman" when I meant
"Romeo". Eeeeeek! Quick-thinkingly I pretended to

have something in my throat, to explain why I was spluttering and going bright red and why the wrong word came out. I didn't put my hand up any more after that – just in case.

When the bell went and we piled out into the corridor I decided to survey Simon Driscott because the *Asking Boys Out* survey was 50% each so far (I am in the middle which is called a floating voter, even though it involves no water at all). I decided not to survey him straight out but to work up to it, because you can freak boys out with emotionality.

So first I casually said, "Simon, do you find it embarrassing to ask people out?"

Simon Driscott went bright red then for some reason and started stammering. I didn't know why for about 18 seconds, and then I realized that I had in fact been very unthoughtful as he has never had a girlfriend that I can remember, and we have been in the same class since we were 5 years old each. So I changed the question to one he would

85

find not embarrassing, which was, "Simon, can you imagine being a girl?"

But he just went even bright redder so I went, "I am not saying that you yourself are like a girl, but that if you *were* an actual girl, would you ask a boy out?"

Simon looked at me with this stare that Mum calls "rabbit caught in the headlights", then went, "Oh, right! Well, I'd have to be pretty sure the boy liked me."

"Okay," I went. "So what about if he had requested a song for you on the radio?"

For some weird reason Simon Driscott suddenly broke out smiling. It was a sort of strange lopsided grin to match his strange lopsided haircut. "Oh, Lucy," he went, "well, erm, if I were a girl, for example, *you,* and that exact thing you just said had happened in the very recent past, for example, *this morning*, I would respond to your question in the affirmative."

I peered at him, going, "Meaning what?"

"Meaning yes," he said, still all stammery. "Yes, I would ask the boy out."

So I went, "Thanks, Simon, you've been massively helpful. I'll ask him right now."

Then there was this strange pause where he looked at me like he thought I was going to say something else. But that was it and he had solved the question, so I just went, "See you around then," and walked off.

As I was almost actually skipping down the corridor I thought how Simon Driscott is an okay boy, even though he is trapped in the body of a geek. I thought how it's so nice, isn't it, that in this day and age (as my nan Delia calls it) boys and girls can be sort of friends (not **BFF** of course, but just normal friends) without fancying each other. Strangely, when I looked round Simon Driscott was making a move to pretend bang his head on the wall. It must be some weird thing out of *Star Trek* I don't understand, like the hand signal thing. Oh well. Boys can be a mystery sometimes.

So, I was going to follow Simon Driscott's and Jules's advice and find Wayne and ask him out that actual minute, but then I realized that *obviously* I had to go and check my hair and make-up first.

Oh! Now I am about to go and ask him, I have just had a **REVELATION**. However nice I look from the neck up, from the neck down I am still covered in the revolting boy-scout green colour of my school uniform. So unless I am going to pop up over a wall and ask Wayne Roman out with just my head showing, I have to do something about my gross-o-matic uniform. I know! I'll wait till Joe's party on Saturday night, when I can wear my new chiffon turquoise top with jeans and some high heels that make me look like an actual teenager instead of a very-nearly one. *(I mainly gaze at my high heels lovingly rather than wear them, 'cos Mum doesn't let me except on special occasions, as she reckons my feet will grow all weird*

and crooked if I wear them every day.
So I will have to change into them right
at the last minute by the door so she
doesn't see and get suspicious that it is a
"special occasion" and not just a Completely
Usual Walk.)

When I think about the party I feel a bit bad
about the Going For a Completely Usual Walk
Plan, 'cos of not telling Mum and Tilda the exact
truth. But then I instantly think of Romeo and
how he went to a party he wasn't allowed to so he
could ask for Juliet's hand, which means getting
married and not just wanting to chop it off and
keep it in a jar or something. In modern-day
language that is like going out because no one gets
married at age 12 any more. So what I'm thinking
is that sometimes you have to be a tiny bit not-
quite-telling-everything if you are in Forbidden
Love. And I'd better not even tell Mum anything
about liking Wayne in case she gets suspicious and
stops us at point number 1 of the plan.

Anyway, it is true that we are going on a walk, and it is true we are only popping into Joe's house for a few minutes, so it's not like we're really properly going to the party anyway. So it's not in fact actual lying, I don't think, so I shouldn't feel bad. And even if we stay for about 15 minutes, that is still only 5 minutes each which is like not hardly going at all. Anyway, we might not bother at all in the end, but I have planned what I am wearing just in case:

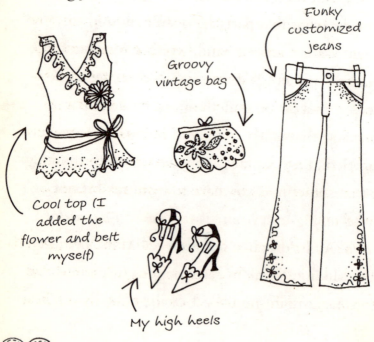

Funky customized jeans

Groovy vintage bag

Cool top (I added the flower and belt myself)

My high heels

## saturday night

before the cool sleepover and
video night we are having,
and maybe the little walk past
Joe's house *wink wink*!!!!

Me and Alex went out with Delia (Nan) today
because Mum was going ice-skating with Gloria.
(Never mind that we wanted to go as well!) Of
course I am old enough to look after Alex on my
own without anyone else there but Mum said no.
Actually it was quite fun with Nan in the end, so
that was okay. We went to the park and 'cos no
one I knew was there I could just go on the swings
properly, instead of standing up or jumping off or
other stuff you do to show you are really too old
for them.

Then we went to the little café and Nan (Delia)
just had a herb tea because coffee gives her *Toilet
Trouble*, which she talked about in totally medical

detail *(yuck!)*. I would have had coffee
if anyone from school was there but I
had a Panda Pop like Alex instead.
I had the lemonade one and he had the
cherry, which were our favourites when we were
children (well, he still is a child, but you know
what I mean).

Dad was right when he said age is weird. I
mean, is he really too old to be a rock star? Am I
really too old to have a Panda Pop? I suppose part
of me is and part of me isn't. I'm sort of stuck in
between. Like, today I didn't even bother with any
make-up 'cos Nan (Delia) lives miles away from
anyone else I know. Plus, I sat on her lap and had a
long cuddle in the café, and when Alex wanted to
come in too I didn't shove him off.

But with Wayne I feel like I've got to be
grown-up and cool and looking nice all the time.
It's scary and exciting that he only knows the Lucy
who I am at school and not the Nan-cuddling,
Panda-Pop-drinking one. And he doesn't know

anything about me as a little kid either, like when I used to melt my Easter eggs on the radiator and remould them into rude shapes.

So anyway I am thinking, which one is the real Lucy? Is it the Lucy in the park today or the Lucy of tonight who is maybe going to an out-of-bounds teenagers' party for about 20 seconds to see the boy she *Forbiddenly Loves*?!

## Sunday afternoon,

sitting in front of our computer, which is so ancient it probably does not even have 20 mega-bites, whatever they are. Feeling sad.

*D*ad has just taken us for our usual walk and mooch round town that he does on a Sunday and *miracle* Mum decided to come as well, instead of staying at home alone and thinking of nothing, as she usually likes to. I invited Dad to the Battle of the Bands Competition to see my Blackstone designs, but he said he is already coming 'cos, "Some wally invited Sally Benson to cover it" and

← *Me, but shhh!!!*

he has to set up her gear and run round after her. He was well grumpy that he has to see her on his day off, "as well as all flaming week" and he also said people shouldn't be allowed pink spiky hairdos, "unless they were there at the heyday of punk, which was before that young lady was even born."

I just went "Yeah" but I'm secretly pleased because having Dad right next to Sally on the night will make it easier for my plan to work.

You might be wondering why I am *feeling sad*. Well, I really want to speak to Tilda but I'm not allowed as it's family day. So instead of ringing her up I have written a letter. I did it typed out on the computer so she will know that I am *officially sorry*. (You will see for what in a minute, 'cos I printed out an extra copy for my journal.) It takes about 27 minutes to print out a simple letter (our printer is ancient) so it is not any good for the demands of the modern world, but I have to make the best of it. This is what I put:

Dear Tilda,

I know you are still not speaking to me after last night, because you did mention that you were in fact NEVER speaking to me for ALL TIME, so I think you were a bit upset. Anyway, I am hoping that while you are ignoring words coming out of my mouth you are not ignoring words I have typed out on paper i.e. these ones. I know it looks like I was a Bad Friend Forever last night, but I have some reasons to explain that I was in fact trying to be a Best Friend Forever.

The reason I didn't tell you about the party is that you would not have come, and as we are all three BFF we HAD to go together. It was not a lie exactly but just not telling the whole information. So it is true that I did know there was a party in Joe's house, but also, Tilda, you have to think of all the things I did not know.

1. I did not know there would be cigarettes.
2. I did not know there would be beer.
3. I did not know JJ would be there.

4. I did not know that, when I was about to ask Wayne Roman out, Gross Foundation Line girl (Tamsin from Year 10) would start having a go at me for no reason. (She's just jealous because she fancies Wayne, BTW, but he doesn't like her 'cos instead he likes me. Well, he did before last night, anyway.)

5. I did not know that while I was in the loo hiding from Tamsin, and Jules was in the coat cupboard hiding from JJ, Jack and Joe persuaded you to join in the mosh and you nearly got squished to actual DEATH.

So, I can sort of understand why you phoned up your dad from Joe's kitchen and got him to come, although it is a shame he got out of the car and walked right into the house because:

1. He looked so furious that his eyes almost popped out of his head and his face was the colour of livid, which is not good for anyone's health.

2. He snapped the stereo off and made a massive fuss about marching us into the car, plus he gave Joe that lecture about Abusing Your Parents' Trust and how he'd better send everyone home this minute and clear up or the POLICE would be involved.

That was completely embarrassing beyond belief. I still have such terrible cringitis I actually want to live the rest of my life under my duvet, but I just know Mum is going to make me go to school tomorrow.

So instead, I am going to live the rest of my life in the girls' loos because there is no way I am facing the band ever again. I have lost the boy I am in Forbidden Love with, and I have lost my first commission in my career as a fashion designer. Plus, our BFF triangle is ruined because Jules is still mad at you. She says you have ruined our image and that Wayne Roman now thinks I am a tiny, weeny infant or maybe even a foetus, i.e., so young I am not even born. So I do understand why you phoned your dad, but also you have ruined three-quarters of my life.

Luckily I have decided to forgive you for this because the only reason you were at the party at all was because of me.

Lots and lots and lots of love from

Lucy xxxxx

PS I totally don't get why you didn't just tell your dad I tricked you into going to the party. Then you would not be in trouble, at least.

Mum has just walked past and I have tried to look really, really as sorry as possible. Tilda is not the only one who is angry with me. When her dad came back here last night with all three of us in the car and told my mum what had happened, she said please could he take Jules home as well, because obviously she needed to talk to me alone, and he said, *Absolutely*. I was completely trembling because she said it in her quiet voice that she hardly ever uses, which is way scarier than her shouty kind of angry.

Then Jules and Tilda got their sleeping-over stuff from upstairs and got back in the car, and I wasn't even allowed to say goodbye to them on the doorstep. I wanted to make myself some hot chocolate, but I didn't even dare do anything apart from sit at the kitchen table.

Mum marched in and went, "Lucy, I can hardly… I'm… How could you…"

I was just silent. The problem was she didn't finish any sentences so I didn't know what to say back. I thought of mentioning that, but it didn't seem like a good idea.

Mum just took a deep breath and went, "I don't think we should talk about this now. Please go to your room."

I didn't argue, even though it was only 10 minutes past 9. I stood up to go and that's when I saw the popcorn she had made for us in a big bowl on the side. My stomach completely flipped over, and I felt utterly sick.

Me and Tilda and Jules were going to get in our sleeping bags and watch *Notting Hill* downstairs with Mum when we came back from the walk. I lurched out of the kitchen holding my stomach, not daring to even look at her. When I got upstairs I crawled right underneath my duvet, even my head, and cried for ages.

Alex was spending time with Mum this morning on his homework project about bees, and then we all had the walk with Dad, so me and Mum haven't been on our own all day.

Oh, no, she's just asked me to come into the kitchen.

## GULP.

Have to go right now…

## Still Sunday,

_after the talk with Mum,_
_still feeling trembly._

**W**hen I went into the kitchen, Mum invited me to sit down, which made me go all sick-feeling again, 'cos normally you can just sit down in your own house without being asked. Then she said this thing really carefully that sounded like she'd been practising it in her head all night, which was, "Lucy, as I'm sure you're aware, the events of last night were completely unacceptable. It's a question of your safety and when I think what could have happened... I assume you didn't ask me for permission to go to the party because you knew I wouldn't allow it. You were right. But I hope you can see now that I would have said no for good reasons."

"I _can_ see that now," I said, really quietly. "But I was only going in for a minute and I honestly had no idea there would be smoking or drinking or—"

"Oh please stop!" said Mum, waving her hands at me. "I can hardly bear to think about it!" She started talking really fast then, sounding like her normal self again and looking right into my eyes. "I know I can't keep you locked in the house, but really, Lu, if something like this comes up again, don't kid yourself that it's okay. I can understand you wanting to find things out for yourself, but sometimes you've just got to trust that I know a little more about life than you do. I mean, only a *tiny* little bit more, but still. Look, things are going to get very sticky round here if you decide that the only way to get what you want is by going behind my back. I'm so hurt that you lied to me, Lu. If this sort of thing happens again, talk to me about it, won't you, and we'll try to come up with some kind of solution."

"I will, I promise," I said, and burst out crying. Suddenly it was like the cool-acting, nearly-teenager Lucy was gone and I just felt like the no-make-up, drinking-Panda-Pops Lucy instead. But I didn't mind. It's been so horrible knowing Mum was so angry with me that I only slept for about 8 minutes all night, and I've spent all day not hardly looking at her. When she pulled me onto her lap and hugged me I just started crying even more.

"Why did it even enter your head to go there, love?" Mum said after a while.

"It was Shakespeare's fault," I sniffled.

Mum looked totally confused and went, "Are we talking about *William* Shakespeare here? The playwright?" I nodded snufflingly and she went, "Lu, it's true that men are to blame for a lot, but you can't pin this on a guy who's been dead for over 300 years."

I smiled a bit about that but then stopped because I wasn't sure if it was okay to look even a tiny bit happy yet. "I mean, he gave me the idea to go to the party," I explained, "'cos, you know, Romeo went to the Capulets' party when he wasn't supposed to."

Mum looked even more utterly confused then,

so I decided to tell her the whole thing, because none of it matters any more. "I am in *Forbidden Love* with Wayne Roman," I said. "He invited me to the party and I decided to go to it so I could ask him out while not wearing a gross-o-matic school uniform."

Mum just blinked at me. "According to *Raising Teenagers – The Most Rewarding Years* this shouldn't be happening for at least another 18 months," she shrieked. "I'm not ready! Please don't do this to me yet, Lu, I don't think I can cope!"

"I'm sorry, but I didn't choose to fall in *Forbidden Love*," I said. "Anyway, you don't have to worry because Wayne'll never speak to me again after Tilda's dad marched in and made me look like a really small child in front of him and all his mates."

"Oh, Lu, I'm sorry," said Mum. "But if it's any consolation it's probably for the best. It would only have ended in tears."

"It already *has* ended in tears," I said. "Mine!" And that started me off crying again.

Mum just hugged me for a really long time. Then she said this thing you will not even believe, which was, "I have to admit that I haven't been quite honest with you about something either. It's no way to set an example, and I'm sorry." Then she told me that when we were over at Nan's and she went ice-skating, instead of being just with Gloria it was with Gloria's boyfriend as well, and his friend called Mike. So it was in fact a double date!!!

I got how hurt she must feel about me lying then, because I felt it myself about her. "But why couldn't you just say?" I asked.

Mum said, "I didn't want to tell you unless something came of it because I didn't know how you'd react."

I tried to pretend I didn't feel completely sick at the idea of Mum with an actual *man* who wasn't Dad. In fact, because they've been getting on better I was even thinking a tiny bit that maybe...but it doesn't matter now. "So, has something come out of it?" I said, trying to sound normal.

Mum smiled a bit sadly. "It was fun, but I realized that I'm not ready to see anyone new yet."

I was so relieved then, and I said all sternly, "You still should have told me before, young lady. It's a question of your safety. I mean, ice-skating can be very dangerous for the elderly!"

Mum said, "Don't be cheeky!" and pretend-spanked me on the bum, and it was okay between us again, but I am still feeling awful nearly every second. I feel awful that I lied to Mum, and awful that the thing with Wayne Roman is over for ever before it even properly started, and awful that Tilda is mad with me and is maybe not even my BFF any more, and awful that Jules is mad with Tilda when it's not really her fault she called her dad, and awful just in general. There is only one little tiny thing I can make better at this exact moment, so I am going to the shop to buy a packet of fruit pastilles. Then Alex can have his green ones back, at least.

## Monday morning
### in the cloakroom.

I just now tried to give the letter I wrote yesterday to Tilda with a packet of crisps but she just flipped her plaits and walked past without even looking what flavour they were. Instead I will put the letter in her bag at breaktime, and the crisps.

To smooth things over from the other side I also said, "Jules, why are you in **SUCH** a big mood with Tilda?" and she just looked all furious and said, "It's up to me what size mood I'm in! It's just lucky for her your mum didn't tell my mum what really happened, or I would be in an even *giganticker* one!"

# Tuesday

after school when I
have just got home.

**W**ell, what I have just got home from is a day
that was ruined by Tilda not talking to me or Jules,
but cheered up by Wayne Roman actually amazingly
still speaking to me! It must be that he really loves
me too and that our *Forbidden Love* conquers
all barriers, even the ones of total complete
embarrassment! I think probably I shouldn't tell
Mum about this until she has finished reading
*Raising Teenagers – The Most Rewarding
Years*, so she is prepared. But then I honestly
will – promise!

I have just got this journal out to write the thing
above about Wayne and I have discovered a letter
from Tilda in my bag. So, although she is still not
speaking to me or handing me things, she is at least
writing to me. Hang on, I just have to open it:

Oh…

Third bench from the playground wall

Tambridge High School

Sherborne

Dorset


Tuesday, 22nd March


Dear Ms. Hartley,

Please note that I am NOT speaking OR writing to you,

therefore kindly refrain from entering into further

correspondence with me.

Yours faithfully,

Matilda-Jane Van der Zwan


   PS It is not withholding information but an actual

lie when someone knows there is a teenage party

happening, but instead says:

We're just going out for a bit of fresh air and exercise, it's not good for your health to sit watching videos all night, and if we just happen to go by Joe's door while he is having a quiet night in with his parents and we just happen to pop in to have a quick professional chat about the band etc. etc.

PPS I shouldn't have believed you when you said that anyway because firstly it is impossible to have a professional chat with Joe and secondly who would just go out for a quick walk in those high heels you were wearing? I can't believe you and Jules got all dressed up but let me go in there just wearing a boring top and no make-up. That is NOT best friendliness!

PPPS Lying to me and putting me in DANGER OF

DEATH in the mosh is not best friendliness either!

PPPPS Re: Your PS, I pretended to Daddy I knew about the party so you didn't get in even more trouble for tricking me, which is true best friendliness.

PPPPPS Jules might be in a mood with me now but she jumped in the car pretty fast when JJ nearly spotted her.

PPPPPPS I know you will say that all these PSs count as writing to you, but technically postscripts are not part of the letter.

PPPPPPPS Where are those crisps you were going to give me earlier?

Oops, I got hungry because of all the stress and sort of ended up eating them.

Tilda said no correspondence, which I think means typed-up letters, but I am going to make her a "*sorry*" card right now which doesn't count. I really want to show her how much I appreciate her **BFF**ness in pretending to her dad that she knew about the party.

# Wednesday

after school.

Well, I didn't think you'd get to see the "sorry" card for Tilda in fact, but sadly you will 'cos she sent it back. BTW, it is cut in half, not 'cos I don't like Tilda but so you can see both bits.

Dear Tilda,

I am sooooooo sorry!
I hope you can forgive me.

Love,
Lucy xxx

PS Anyway, the good news is you
can now stop feeling so bad for
ruining my life as by a miracle Wayne
Roman is still actually speaking to
me and so are Joe Black and Jack
Stone. So I am still going to ask out
Wayne Roman.

There was also this note from her in it:

Outside the music centre waiting

for my piano lesson

Tambridge High School

Sherborne

Dorset

Wednesday, 23rd March

Dear Ms. Hartley,

Why are you still writing to me when I am not writing

back?

Yours,

Matilda-Jane Van der Zwan

PS Cards count as correspondence actually.

PPS In reply to your "good news" that I can stop

feeling bad, I never felt bad in the first place, so how can I not feel bad any more? It is you who should feel bad!

PPPS I do not believe you would give me your Juicy Jelly lipgloss to prove you are sorry, otherwise you would have put it in with this card.

PPPPS I have to say this because I am worried about you, and deep, deep, deep down underneath how angry I am you are still my friend. PLEASE don't ask Wayne Roman out, Lucy, please, please, please!!! He is Bad News and also too old for you.

Oh no! I really *really* don't want to upset Tilda any more but I really really *really* want to ask Wayne Roman out, and I will – I'm going to get him to meet me in the old music room after lunch and ask him then. Hey, I know – maybe when me and Wayne get married and stay together for about 20 years Tilda will see that we are happy and say, "Wow, Lucy, your love has lasted long even though it started off star-crossed like in Shakespeare," and then she will realize she was wrong and say sorry, and it will be *her* buying *me* bacon crisps in actual fact.

## Thursday lunchtime

in the loos locked in
a cubicle by myself.

Something totally awful has just happened and I
am still shaking from it. Oh, I think I am too upset
to write about it and I will just have a cry instead.

## After school on Thursday

okay, now I can tell you about it.

Well, first what happened was that after lunch was
our computer lesson so I had to get out of the
toilet cubicle and dry my eyes and blow my nose
and go over to the science block, where the
computer room also is.

Even though I tried to quickly clean up the
mascara that was running down my face I must

have looked really upset from what happened. We were all on separate computers and we were supposed to be researching the individual topics we are doing reports on. We are supposed to go on the Internet and find information and then make it into a report by editing nicely and adding bits we have found from the library in books. What me and Jules and Tilda usually do instead is e-mail each other, because Mr. Webster, who is the student teacher, mainly reads and leaves us alone as long as we are quiet.

Mr. Webster's preferred reading

I put my computer on and there was this e-mail from Tilda, and then I did quite a long reply. I have just now printed them both off from my computer at home to save trying to remember exactly what it said.

**To:** <u>fashiongoddess17@hotmail.com</u>

**From:** <u>vanderzwanfamily@ntlhome.com</u>

**Subject:** There isn't one.

---

Dear Lucy,

I am still not speaking or writing or even e-mailing to you.

Tilda

PS Are you okay? I am worried because you look not okay. xx

I did this reply and copied it to Jules 'cos she looked worried too.

**To:** princessofdarkness9@yahoo.com;

vanderzwanfamily@ntlhome.com

**From:** fashiongoddess17@hotmail.com

**Subject:** My upsetness

---

No, I am not really okay, 'cos, well, as you (meaning Jules) will know, and as you (meaning Tilda) won't know, I was meeting Wayne Roman in the old music room after lunch, just me and him, because I was going to ask him out (sorry, Tilda).

Well, he got there and he said more things like how beautiful and wonderful I am and how nice it was to have some time on our own for once. He was talking about how maybe my dad could get Blackstone in to do a session like they do on Radio 1 where you play 3 songs and have a sort of interview chat thing in between and that. Plus he said how he listened to Wicked Fm for one whole week and he didn't hear my dad's show and when was it exactly?

Anyway, to take the subject off the DJ thing

(which I will explain about later) I decided it was the moment to ask THE QUESTION.

I went, "Wayne, there's something I want to..."

But just then that girl Tamsin walked in.

The amount of times she has been nasty to me had made me decide to not bother being nice to her so I said, "Do you mind? We're having a private conversation."

Wayne was giving her this straining look, like he was trying to tell her something using only psychic-ness. I thought he was trying to say "Go away", but in fact the look was for a different reason, which I will tell you in a minute.

Tamsin just gave me this really smug look and went, "There's nothing you can say to him that you can't say to me."

I was trying to use my own psychic-ness to think at her "Go away, go away, go away", but it didn't work so I said, "Why not?"

Then Tamsin said the bombshell, which was, "Because he's MY BOYFRIEND."

I have now realized that I should have used the

swaying walk I learned on the runway at London Fashion Week to glide straight out of the room with my nose in the air and my dignity in one piece. But instead this totally embarrassing thing slipped out of my mouth, which was, "But Wayne, you like ME. Or otherwise why would you hint that you did outside science, and why would you call me beautiful and wonderful not once, but actually twice, and also why would you request Blackstone's song on the radio for me?"

Wayne blinked at me and Tamsin glared at him. "What song?" they both said at the same time, with her sounding angry and him sounding confused. How confused he sounded made me know right away that he didn't request it for me after all, so I just said, "Never mind."

Tamsin said to him, "Well, what about all the other stuff, and don't deny it because I have seen you hugging HER and flirting with HER and spending your breaktimes alone with HER when you said it was the whole band. I've been an idiot to think it was nothing when you obviously fancy HER."

Wayne went deadly pale, and that's when I knew for

definite it was true about Tamsin going out with him. I was too upset to speak, but sadly I was not too upset to listen. Wayne was going, "Please, Tam, it's not like you think. I don't fancy her. Yeah, right, me and a Year 8, give me some credit! I was just letting her think I did 'cos her dad's a DJ at Wicked FM, and I wanted to get some airtime for the band."

So that explains why he was all of a sudden nice to me after they came over, not 'cos of the spell but 'cos of him thinking my dad is a DJ (PROMISE will tell you later) and also why he was still nice to me even after the party embarrassment.

I don't know what happened then 'cos my eyes were all blurry from tears, and I ran away 'cos I have never felt more completely stupid in my whole entire life. So please, PLEASE will you two stop fighting with each other over that stupid party thing that was all my fault anyway and come and hug me because I need you right now.

Love from your BFF (I hope, Tilda),

Lucy xxxxx

Suddenly they both got up and came over to me.

Jules was saying, "Grr, I'll get JJ to punch Wayne in for you."

I was saying, "That's okay, thanks, because I wouldn't want JJ to get in trouble, and instead I am going to do a spell on Wayne Roman to turn him into the slug he is."

Tilda said, "Sorry for still not speaking to you when something really bad has happened."

I said, "That's okay, you didn't know."

Jules said, "Sorry, Tilda, for being in a mood after the party."

Tilda said, "Sorry, Jules, for panicking and phoning my dad."

But it was all really quick and talking over each other, so no one but us would have known what we were on about. Then we all started having a huggy, squealing, crying, making-up session right in the middle of the room.

Mr. Webster was staring and blinking at us, having absolutely no idea what had happened, and everyone else was staring at him to see what he would do about us. But he didn't do anything about us because that was when Mrs. Stepton came in from the science room next door and went, "What's going on, Mr. Webster?"

I stopped crying and Jules stopped shouting and Tilda stopped squealing right then.

Mr. Webster covered his magazine up with a file and went, "I honestly don't know. One minute these girls were quietly researching their individual topic reports on the computer and then…this…"

Mrs. Stepton peered at me and went, "Hmm." Then she looked at the nearest empty computer, which was Tilda's, which of course still had the e-mail from me open on it.

Then she started reading it out in front of the whole entire class, like: "*Well, as you (meaning Jules) will know…*"

I thought I was going to die right there and then of a giant attack of *cringitis*, but then she frowned and peered at the screen and started reading in her head. Everyone was quiet and pretending to get on with their work because Mrs. Stepton can be quite stern, but I knew that really they were waiting too. Then she looked up and went, "Whose work is this?"

Tilda put her hand up shakily. I felt *soooooo* sorry for her because I thought she was going to get in mega-trouble *again* even though it wasn't her fault *again*.

But Mrs. Stepton smiled and just said, "A very good report, Tilda. I have no idea what you girls were creating such a commotion about, but it's time to get back on with your work."

"Yes, Mrs. Stepton," we all said at once, looking amazed that she didn't tell us off for e-mailing in computers.

"And what do you girls say to Mr. Webster?"

"Sorry, Mr. Webster," we all said like a chorus.

"Right then," said Mrs. Stepton, giving me an intense look that I didn't really understand.

"That's sorted that out then. Now, I must get back next door or my own lot will probably blow themselves up. And do remember, Lucy, if you ever want to discuss the contents of *your* – ahem – individual topic report, my door is always open."

And then she went. And then Mr. Webster gave me this look like: *Why would you want to discuss your report with her?* and I did this shrug like: *Who knows?* and got quickly back to my computer and my report about William Shakespeare. Suddenly I didn't feel like doing it about him any more, after what happened with Wayne Roman, so instead I have started doing it about Stella Boyd, who is the totally fab fashion designer I recently met.

So at least me and Tilda and Jules all made up again, which means that something good has come out of all the *adversity*. Also, at last break Tamsin came up to me and I thought *Eeeeeek!* she is going to have a go at me in front of my new reunited BFF and actually Jules was all ready to have a go back. But instead she said how she thought Wayne was a pig for doing that to me, and she doesn't want to go out with a pig, and so she has in fact chucked him! She said she was sorry for being mean to me, but she thought I was trying to take her boyfriend away.

I went, "Wow, you really thought I could take Wayne Roman off you and go out with him?"

And she said, "Yeah, of course. I only said that stuff about you being a kid because I was scared he'd go off with you."

And so then I was a tiny bit cheered up because at least Tamsin thought I was proper competition and not just a tiny foetus fan following Wayne around.

I had to tell Tilda and Jules about the Dad being a DJ misunderstanding straight after computers because I said about it in my e-mail. I thought they would be annoyed with me for not telling Wayne and them lot the truth but they didn't mind. I even told them about the *Mad Fan*

*Plan.* I was so annoyed at Wayne I felt like telling Sally Benson the concert is cancelled so don't bother coming, but Tilda pointed out that that will spoil it for Joe Black and Jack Stone and even more for Dad, so I am just going to have to live with the revolting Wayne getting on the radio too.

After school I was still really upset so Jules walked all the way back with me and delivered me to Mum. Then Jules went, and Mum made me a hot chocolate even though it was only 4.15, and I told her all about how Wayne liked me again after the party, and how I tried to ask him out and it all went wrong. "I was so sure he liked me, with the song and the pendulum and the spell and everything," I said snifflingly. "I thought it was my first time in love."

Mum hugged me tight and said wisely, "Well, when it comes to love you can look at your stars and palm and tea leaves all you like and miss the blindingly obvious."

So I went, "Well, the blindingly obvious now is that I can't go to the Battle of the Bands because I can't stand to see Wayne Roman ever, ever, ever again."

Mum got all stern then. "You jolly well *are* going, young lady," she said. "No silly boy is spoiling your big moment when you and the girls have worked so hard on customizing the band's outfits. And anyway, Alex and I are coming to see what you've done and then we've all been invited to Jules's house afterwards."

Well, Isabella and Gabriel's family parties are the best fun ever with paella and salsa dancing and shouty games like charades, and there is no way I am missing one just for stupid Wayne, so that is that decided.

Wow, my mum is a total Stand-up Babe – that must be where I get it from!

# Friday

*after school.*

**W**ell, last night after I had cheered up a tiny bit I looked at my Teen Witch Kit for spells to get revenge on Wayne Roman. I was hoping I could make him get a huge pulsating spot or an allergy to rugby, or even something more traditional like turning him into a frog. But it just said:

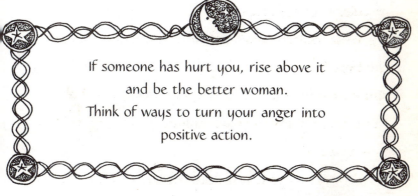

If someone has hurt you, rise above it and be the better woman.
Think of ways to turn your anger into positive action.

And suddenly I thought of a brilliant way to be better than Wayne! My plan is to not just be a better person on the inside than him but to be *actually* better on the outside, as in:

# The Positive Action Revenge on Wayne Roman Plan

1. Me and Jules and Tilda make our own band and write a song and everything.
2. We enter into the Battle of the Bands Competition and win.
3. Wayne Roman loses, plus he sees me strutting my funky stuff onstage.
4. Wayne Roman has a **REVELATION** that he does actually fancy me, but knows that I will never, ever go out with him, not in a million years.
5. Wayne Roman's heart breaks loudly, like **CRACK!!!** and he knows how I feel.

## HA-HA-HAAAAAA!

Evil-genius laugh! ⟶

At first break in the loos I told the girls about my plan. Jules is going to sing with me, and Tilda is going to do the keyboards. We are all mega-excited!!!

Tonight we are each going to try and come up with a song, and tomorrow they are coming round to mine. I have said to bring their most groovy gear so I can put our outfits together like I did with Blackstone. Wow, I am starting to feel happy again. This is going to be *soooooo* cool and so totally serving right to Wayne Roman.

## Saturday evening
just before the Battle of
the Bands. Eeeeeek!!!

Well, Jules came round quite early, like say about
9.30 a.m. in the morning because there was a lot
to do. She brought JJ's guitar even though she only
knows 3 chords on it. Hopefully they will be the
ones in the song because knowing Jules she will
play them anyway, and it will be a racket.

Then there was another ring on the door,
which was Tilda being dropped off with her
keyboard.

I got totally excited about tonight, like leaping
round going "Yee-hah, Grandma!"

But then we got the terrible news that Tilda
isn't allowed to perform. She is banned from
playing in the concert as a punishment because of
going to the party.

I went, "You mean, you still haven't told your

dad it was me and Jules's fault you even went there?"

Tilda shook her head. "No. As I said, I have to pretend I knew as well. If I tell him you tricked me into it then he might stop me from seeing you, and anyway, **BFF** stick together."

I felt like slugweed then because in trying to make us stick together physically by going to the party I had unstuck us emotionality-wise by not telling Tilda the truth. Wow, I am so lucky to have her for a **BFF**. But the way I felt really bad must have still shown on my face 'cos Tilda said, "No way would I be brave enough to go onstage in front of people anyway, so it doesn't make any difference. I go all shy and my voice goes like wobbly jelly, like in choir."

Jules said, "Yeah, it's a bit wobbly." We were both remembering Tilda singing **BRILLIANTLY** in the old music room, but there is no point saying about that because at the Battle of the Bands there would be tons of audience watching her.

"Well, at least you'll be there to support us," I said.

But Tilda shook her head sadly. "No I won't. My dad had to go to London for some emergency work thing, and he's asked your mum to drop me home before the concert, 'cos he'll be back then."

"Oh," went me and Jules, in total disappointment.

We decided that Tilda is going to make up the music and record it for us so we can just play it back over the sound system. So she will sort of be there, spiritually anyway.

I am *soooooo* over Wayne now that last night I could even concentrate on writing a song. (Tilda and Jules are also completely over him, in support of me.) It is called "Love Rat" and is to the same music as "Love Shack". It is about this fictional boy I made up who is a Love Rat. He acts like he fancies this girl to get onto a TV show her dad presents, but really he already has a girlfriend.

When I did it for Tilda and Jules, Jules said,

138

"Wow, Lucy, you are scary!"

Tilda said, "It's cool, but what you have actually done is written a whole song about Wayne."

I realized then that she was right, and I didn't want *our* song to be about *him*, yuck! Tilda hadn't written a song because she had to do all her weekend homework last night to be allowed round here today. But luckily Jules had done one. She said it was inspired by what Tilda said yesterday about **BFF** sticking together.

Jules's song is called "Cheese Sandwich" and it goes like this:

No one's gonna stop me from
Being myself totally
Even when I'm all grown up
I'll still have a cheese sandwich
when I want
Don't worry 'cos I've got
My pals, my posse, my crew

139

*They really love me*
*I know they do*
*BFF means Best Friends Forever*
*BFF means sticking together*
*They'll get you through all the pain and*
*sadness and death in this world, the*
*meaningless war and unnecessary*
*starvation and...*

I stopped her then because the lyrics had gone a bit heavy. I said, "We love it but how about just repeating the **BFF** bit and then going 'Yeah, yeah, yeah'?"

Jules got instantly moody and went, "What's wrong with the death and pain and sadness bit? It's all true!"

I thought really quickly and said, "That bit is strong enough to be a whole separate song in itself, so you should save it till you learn some more chords." And then Jules was happy again.

While Jules was having an actual cheese

sandwich, Tilda came up with this brill tune on her keyboard. She's done it in this certain key so that Jules can do her 3 chords for the whole song and we have recorded it onto a tape 'cos Tilda can't play live *(sob, sob!!!)*. My singing will be all on its own except maybe I will have a tambourine from the box at school.

Then we had our first practice and it was terrible, but fun, but also sad. I think this is another irony-thingy that the song is about us three **BFF** sticking together and we will not be actually together singing it.

Still, we all had fun sorting out what stuff to wear onstage. Jules went total rock chick overload like this:

And I went seriously funky, like this:

I also helped Tilda style
her cords and top with
accessories, and we put big
silk flowers from Mum's vase
in the hall on my floppy
velvet hat to make a cool
outfit which is in her funky
vintage style so she didn't
feel left out, like this:

A lot of practising and a lot of hours and cheese sandwiches later, we were sounding quite a lot better, although to be honest Jules's voice is a bit screechy. Still, at least she belts it out loudly because she is so confident, so no one will hear me all that much. I am okay, but I keep wanting to sound really special and professionally good like Tilda when we secretly heard her and I really do **NOT** sound like that, so that is a bit disappointing.

Then Mum made us a quick early tea, and afterwards we did our song for her. It was cool because Tilda was actually playing the keyboard even if she wouldn't sing, so we were all three together in front of one person at least.

Instead of doing a massive clap Mum just smiled at the end and said, "There's one thing you're missing, girls." I actually thought she was going to say *talent* because quite honestly we are not that great, but then she went up to the bathroom and came back with…

…her grey shimmery **MAC** eyeshadow!!!

She put it matching on all of us even though Tilda wasn't going to be onstage. Then she said, "Right. Let's go get 'em."

But we didn't go get 'em straight away because suddenly the phone rang. Mum was going, "Hmm, yes, hmm, but I'm sure you don't want me to leave her here on her own. Well, I really do have to take Lucy and Jules to the concert… Hmm, I understand but… No, I'm afraid not as Jules's entire family will also be there…"

I was thinking, I hope I am right about what I am thinking about what is happening…and then Mum put the phone down and I *knew* I was right! Tilda's dad is stuck on the motorway coming back from London so she has to come to the concert with us instead of being dropped off at home, 'cos she's not allowed to be there on her own. Mr. Van der Zwan said he will try to get to the school as soon as possible to collect her. I hope he will be stuck for a very long time, like

144

maybe even the whole thing! At least Tilda will be able to watch us even though she's not allowed to be in it.

Mum said that we didn't have to go quite yet because of Tilda not being taken home, so I am quickly writing this now, while Tilda and Jules are watching the end of *Buffy*. Oh, no I'm not. Amazingly 20 whole minutes have vanished and I have to stop 'cos we are getting in the car. Wish us luck!!!

LUCKY CLOVER!

very late because I am still
too EXCITED to sleep.

**W**ell, I have to write down about tonight, even
though it is 1.32 a.m. in the morning, 'cos then
maybe my head will stop buzzing with the millions
of thoughts of what has happened. I will try to say
it in the right order and not miss anything out, but
there was so much amazingness that I can't
promise you, to be honest.

Well, when we got to the hall Simon Driscott
and the Geeky Minions were setting up the
technicalities with Mr. Wright. My dad was there
organizing Sally Benson's gear, with a big moody
face on. Some people from other schools were
already there, like the Cheston High lot and the
boys from King Alfred's, with their parents and a
few teachers, but the St. Cecilia's girls came in just
with some nuns because it is boarding.

We looked at the list of who was going on when, which was roughly like this:

## Battle of the Bands
## Order of Appearance

1. It's Not Cricket
2. The Diva Sisters
3. Honey Harper ← *Her actual name's Honey – how cool!*
4. Max and Dev
5. The Blingin' Girls Crew Posse
6. Gods of Rock ← *Huh! Pale Weedy Boys of Rock, more like!*
7. Headrush
8. The Red Poncho Bros Peruvian Pan Pipe Band
9. Get Lucky ← *Surprisingly they were not bad!*
10. Steeler ← *Steel drums! Mad or what!*
11. Death Bravado feat. Dictator Potato ←
12. The Young Ladies of St. Cecilia's Convent School
13. Blackstone
14. The BFF

*Dictator Potato was an actual potato. I totally did not get it, but those Cranbourne Theatre Arts School kids thought it was hilaaaarious!!*

Blackstone were actually last, but then we were written in biro after that, because I only told Mr. Wright about us yesterday. We decided to be called The BFF in the end, even though Jules still reckons we should have been called The Cheese Sandwiches.

Then Jules's family all came in and there was lots of hugging and fast talking and then they all got in a row near the front with my mum and Alex. Isabella started pouring out Coke into little plastic cups and handing round cold tortilla sandwiches (which are basically potatoes inside eggs inside bread and which I think are totally gross, BTW).

Just right then, Miss Spiky Pink Head Sally Benson from WICKED FM turned up and headed over to Dad. I am trying this new honesty thing after the terrible party stuff with Mum so instead of doing the Mad Fan Plan I called off the Geeky Minions, and I just stopped her midway and said straight out who I was. I explained how it was me who had invited her and not Jules. Then I really politely asked her if Dad could have a go of the microphone right at the end, just for 5 minutes. I said, "I think he could be a really talented DJ, and I wish he could have a chance to prove it to Robert Hyde."

Sally looked surprisedly at me, but then she said she wouldn't give Dad a chance because it's more than her job's worth and plus he is too old. She made me so furious I almost decided to still do the Mad Fan Plan on her, but I can't stand to get in any more trouble with Mum. Huh! Maybe the saying is wrong about Honesty is the best policy. Actually, maybe setting the Geeky Minions on people is the best policy.

So, I was really mad about Sally Benson not helping 'cos it meant Dad wouldn't get a chance to show his DJ skills, but then the concert kicked off with Sally announcing these posh boys called It's Not Cricket, who sang a miserable thing about, like, politics or something. The hall was so full that

149

me and Tilda and Jules had to stand by the side and Dad came and stood with us as well. He was more staring annoyedly at Sally Benson than listening to the band, and I knew there was no point telling him that I'd invited her and why, not unless she suddenly changed her mind.

To try making Sally suddenly change her mind, I kept giving her pleading looks between each band, but she kept completely ignoring me totally on purpose, and introducing people herself without giving Dad a go. The only good thing was that Tilda's dad didn't turn up so she got to stay with us for all that time.

It was really near the end when the St. Cecilia's girls got up onstage. They all sat down on chairs and got these recorders out, and it looked like we were in for a really yawn-making 5 minutes. But then suddenly this Britney Spears music came blaring out and they whipped off their coats and underneath they had their school uniforms on but all jazzy with the skirts rolled up and the shirts

knotted at the front and stuff. Then they did this
really rude dance with the chairs like Britney does
in the video and one of the nuns'
headdress things actually fell off
with the shock.

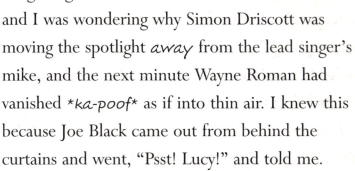

Then the most amazing
thing happened. One minute
Blackstone were waiting in the
wings to go on after St. Cecilia's,
and I was wondering why Simon Driscott was
moving the spotlight *away* from the lead singer's
mike, and the next minute Wayne Roman had
vanished *ka-poof* as if into thin air. I knew this
because Joe Black came out from behind the
curtains and went, "Psst! Lucy!" and told me.

The disappearingness of Wayne only stayed
mysterious until I heard one of the nuns say that 3
of the St. Cecilia's girls had gone missing. After
that it was very simple to work out. As the nuns
went off to look for the girls, Mr. Wright and
Simon Driscott came over. Mr. Wright said,

"What is going on?" in an urgent whisper, and so I did some quick thinking and said that Wayne had suddenly got laryngitis and had to get rushed home, but we were just that second getting a replacement singer.

The audience were all shuffling and whispering so Mr. Wright said he would go and do his monologue from *Henry the Fifth* to entertain them, which is another Shakespeare thing, and we had to "Hurry up and sort this mess out before our school looks completely stupid in front of all these people".

"Right, I'll do it," said Jules. "I'm the right image and everything," and she started marching off onto the stage.

I went, "No, wait! Sorry, Jules, but to be honest you are not all that good, and Blackstone is our school's only chance of winning."

"What about *The BFF*?" Jules hissed moodily.

"Let's face it, we try hard but we are not actually that great," I said, and Jules had to admit I was right. Then I took a deep breath and whispered, "Tilda, you'll have to forget about your nerves and sing, okay? I know you can 'cos we secretly heard you in the old music room."

We were going to never reveal that we knew about Tilda's singing, but we had to 'cos it was a complete emergency. Tilda did the look that Mum calls *rabbit caught in the headlights*. Her voice was all squeaky and stammery and she went, "But there's no way I can sing well in front of people – you *know* that! And what if my dad comes in? I'm banned from being in the concert, remember?"

I was getting upset then because I really wanted everyone to see my Blackstone costumes, especially Mum and Dad and Alex. Plus, Jules was getting upset because I said she was too rubbish to sing on her own, and Tilda was getting upset because she wanted to help but she wouldn't go onstage.

Simon Driscott was the only one not getting upset, which was lucky because he came up with a sudden good idea. He said, "Jules is the right image

153

for the band and she's confident – she could pretend to sing but Tilda could stand backstage and actually sing and I could make her voice come out of the speakers instead of Jules's and no one would know."

I was massively impressed and I was going, "Wow, can you really do that? You're amazing!"

Simon looked totally pleased, probably because I had complimented him on his *technologicality*.

Tilda said okay as long as no one was watching, Simon got on with the technical bit and Jules went onstage with the band.

In a last ditch attempt to get Dad on air I dashed over and quickly told him why I had really invited Sally Benson, but how she wouldn't let him go on air.

Dad smiled and squeezed my hand. "You're a gem, Lu. Let's ask her one more time, both together, and maybe, well, it's worth a try."

Just then, Mr. Wright stopped doing his *Henry the Fifth* and got a big clap. He thought

154

it was because the audience liked it but I secretly think it was because he had stopped at last.

So we asked but Sally Benson still said no, even though Dad said how his *own* daughter designed the *actual* costumes for the band. Instead she just introduced Blackstone herself. God, she is *soooooo* horrible!

The curtains opened again and everyone clapped. Jules looked absolutely **BRILLIANT** in her Goth Rock Chick style, and she went completely *wiiiiiiiiild* onstage. Joe Black and Jack Stone looked great in their gear too, and lots of people congratulated me, so I'm not being big-headed, but only telling the factual truth. But the main thing was that Tilda sounded **AMAZING**. She was obviously completely rocking out hidden behind the curtain because her voice was clear and strong, and she sounded like a real rock star.

Luckily Tilda had spent ages miming the song when me and Jules were singing it round the school, so she knew all the words.

This is my idea of what Tilda
looked like

I was just thinking *phew* about us solving
the disaster of Wayne vanishing, when Mr. Van der
Zwan walked in. He came up to me and asked
where Tilda was. I told him she was in the loos
because there is being honest, and then there is
dropping your **BFF** in the poop, which I did not
want to do. Lucky for us that we hid her behind
the curtain, I was thinking.

The song ended and everyone started clapping and cheering really crazily, because with Tilda's voice and Jules's performance, Blackstone were totally the best thing so far. They were so good, and they so involved Jules and Tilda and so did *not* involve Wayne now, that I really wanted them to win.

Then I saw Jules give a signal to Simon Driscott, and her mike did a squeaking thing and her own actual voice came out, saying, "Ladies and gentlemen, there is another member of the band. She was the one *really* singing just now, but she's too shy to perform in front of anyone."

I was psychically thinking, *Jules! No!*

But suddenly Jules pulled the curtain back, and everyone saw Tilda. They all started clapping and cheering again so she came forward and bowed shyly.

First Tilda's dad looked at her, and then he looked at me, and then his face went the colour of livid and his eyes nearly popped out of his head, like when he walked into Joe's party. But Tilda didn't see him. She was looking really happy by then, beaming a big smile until — **BOOM!!!** — she suddenly spotted him, and went really bright red and ran offstage.

Jules ran after her, and they both came dashing up to me and Mr. Van der Zwan and Dad.

Jules was going to Tilda, "I'm sorry, I didn't know he was here and I thought you should get the credit for your great voice and…"

But Tilda wasn't listening 'cos she was going to her dad, "I'm so sorry, I didn't mean to be in it, it was at the last minute and an emergency and…"

And her dad was angrily saying to her, "How could you disobey me like this? I thought you understood my reasons for banning you from the concert…"

Then Sally Benson announced the next act, which was *The BFF*.

"That's us," I said to Jules. We hugged Tilda with an extra squeeze, meaning *Hope you sort this out*.

158

"Good luck, love," said Dad.

"What are you girls doing?" asked Mr. Van der Zwan.

"We're onstage," I said. "**BFF** stands for Best Friends Forever. It was meant to have Tilda in it as well, because we're a three, but she's too shy and plus, not allowed."

Tilda said then, "I'm not too shy any more. Not now I know everyone likes my voice. Dad, please can I be in it?"

Mr. Van der Zwan looked really sad. "I would love to allow it. But I have to stick to what I said about your punishment. If I start going back on things now…"

That's when I realized that I had to tell him the truth, even if it would make me get in more trouble, because that is what a **BFF** should do. I went, "It was me that made Tilda go to the party, she didn't even know there was one. I tricked her into it because I knew she would never come otherwise. She's just been covering for me so

159

I don't get in more trouble – which I will now, but I'm ready to take it. Honestly, none of this is her fault, and please can she sing, please!"

Mr. Van der Zwan said, "Tilda, is this true?"

She nodded then, and all of us held our breath 'cos we didn't know if that would make things better or worse.

Just then Sally Benson said, "No **BFF**? Okay then, kids, here's the latest from Purple Seven while the judges make their decision."

It was too late. But then Mr. Van der Zwan said, "In that case, young lady, I insist you get up there and enjoy yourself."

I shouted, "Wait! We're here!" and we all grabbed hands and rushed onstage. Simon Driscott quickly set up the keyboard as well, with another mike, so that Tilda could play and sing live.

Well, for the audience it was pretty terrible, to be honest. Luckily we had Tilda's singing, because I only sounded okay and Jules was quite bad, plus, she did the wrong chords on the guitar.

Tilda missed coming in for the second verse on the keyboard, and I tried to swing my hair about in a funky way and ended up hitting myself in the eye – *ow*! But for us three it was the most amazing, breathtaking and brilliant thing. That is because we were up there all together, singing about being **BFF**, which we never thought we would do. And it was even better because we were just doing it for ourselves and not to get *Positive Action Revenge* on Wayne!

When we finished there was a big clap and cheer (luckily Jules has such a big family!) and we had the most amazing surprise. It was Dad's voice on the mike! He had grabbed it off Sally and was going, "Big it up for the fabulicious **BFF** from Tambridge High! The girls only put their band together today, and I'm sure you'll agree with me that they did a great job in the time they had. As well as performing onstage, Jules wrote the song, Tilda composed the music, and my daughter Lucy did the styling. I'm so proud of you, Lu! It seems like just the other day when you used to melt your Easter eggs on the radiator and then remould them into… Anyway, ahem, it's been a great event and as well as raising money for the N.S.P.C.C. we've seen lots of new talent too! Now, in one second Sally will grab this mike back, and tomorrow I'll get the sack, but here's Purple Seven while we wait for the judges' decision."

I just can't believe Dad actually took the chance and did it! And he was brill, too, apart from the bit about my Easter eggs…lucky he stopped right then!

Then the curtain came down and me and Jules and Tilda had a big hug. Then Simon Driscott walked over so we grabbed him and hugged him too, making him go completely red – probably he has never hugged one singular girl before, never mind three at once! Then Jules went to see her parents, and Tilda went to find her dad, and I was just going to see mine as well when Simon Driscott said, "Lucy, I just wanted to say, I'm sorry things didn't work out with Wayne."

I stopped dead and turned back around and stared at him. "How did you know about that?" I stammered, because I thought it was mainly secret.

He shrugged and went, "Erm, the whole school kind of knows."

Oh, *goodie*, I thought.

"I must confess to being disappointed in you, though," he went on. "I mean, Wayne Roman? I thought you were a woman of substance, Lucy."

I peered at him, going, "Are you saying I'm fat?"

He shrugged and went, "Oh forget it!" and did that fake head-banging-on-the-wall thing again. Honestly, what is UP with that?!

"Oh well, it doesn't matter now," I said. "And by the way, I've worked out who sent me the song on the radio."

Simon Driscott got this strange expression on his face then, as if a Brussels sprout had gone down the wrong way. "Really?" he croaked.

"Yeah. It was Dad, of course. I should have realized earlier. The reason the band decided to cover it in the first place is that Wayne found it in Dad's CD collection. It's one of his favourite songs."

"Oh right, yeah," said Simon, looking okay again (well, as okay as you can look with such a lopsided haircut, but at least he had stopped nearly choking).

Anyway, then it was time to announce the

winner and all the bands had to go onstage. Me and Jules and Tilda held hands nervously, like they do on *Pop Idol*. Mr. Wright said, "In third place…Death Bravado featuring Dictator Potato."

Weird, I suppose the judges must have got their kind of humour. They went up and pretended the potato was accepting their prize, which was hidden in an envelope.

"In second place…The Girls Blingin' Crew Posse!" We looked at each other. ↖
We had either won first prize or we weren't in it at all.

*I can't remember exactly what they were called*

When all of the Blingin' Crew Posse of Girls or whatever they were had stomped offstage it went all of a hush again. We gripped hands really tight and squeezed our eyes shut and Mr. Wright said, "…and the winner is…Blackstone!"

Me and Jules and Tilda all screamed (of course we wanted Blackstone to win. We knew realisticly-wise that *The BFF* had no likelyness!), and even Joe and Jack looked a bit pleased instead of just bored. I wasn't going to go up with those 4 to get the prize, but Jules said, "Of course you are, you're the style coordinator," and so I did.

While we were getting the prize (it turned out to be record shop vouchers in the envelopes – how cool!) I saw Wayne Roman being escorted back into the hall by two cross-looking nuns. He didn't look that happy about us winning without him, plus he will be in serious trouble with Mr. Wright about the St. Cecilia's girls. It was strange, but in actual fact I felt sorry for him. Only a tiny weeny bit, though.

Okay, I think I can sleep now I've got all that exciting stuff out of my head. Oh, hang on, maybe I'll just tell you about th

## Sunday morning!

Can you believe I fell asleep
while actually in the middle
of telling you about the
concert! I now have an imprint
of my pen on my cheek!

So anyway, to carry on, we all went round to
Jules's afterwards, including Tilda and her dad, for
a big supper. Tilda's dad has decided to think I am
brave for owning up, instead of bad for tricking
Tilda in the first place, so that is very *very* lucky
for the future of us staying all three together.

How weird that we formed the **BFF** band to
beat Wayne Roman, and in the end he wasn't even
in the concert. I reckon it's another one of those
irony things we did in English. It is also amazing
that in the end I wanted Blackstone to win more
than us. That's 'cos I realized our band was not
meant to be for winning, or even for getting

167

*Positive Action Revenge* on Wayne Roman, but for us doing something all together.

Just when my brain was getting in a knot thinking of all this, Dad walked by with some of those yummy "tappers" things that Jules's mum and dad make because they are Spanish. I nicked one out of his hand and said, "Hey, great job on grabbing the mike, but what made you do that all of a sudden?"

Dad slapped my hand away from taking another bit of his food and went, "Well, *you* did actually. There I was, standing right next to you, and I heard you owning up to Mr. Van der Zwan. You took a risk even though it could have landed you in even more trouble. So I decided to take a risk too."

So then I was thinking, *Wow! I have actually inspired my own dad!*

**BTW**, I told him how I was worried about Mum finding out what I did to Tilda with the party thing, because I feel so awful about it, which

I totally do. So he had a word with Mr. Van der Zwan and they decided that there's no need to tell Mum, at least not till she's finished reading *Raising Teenagers – The Most Rewarding Years.*

Just at that moment when we were talking, Dad's mobile rang. "Here we go," he said, showing me the screen, which said "The Boss" for who was calling. "Time to face the music, ha ha."

I just heard little bits when Dad moved the phone away from his ear, like, "completely unprofessional" and "Sally was absolutely furious" but then I heard "admire your *chutzpah*" and I tried to ask Dad what it meant but he just went, "Shhh!" and clamped the phone to his ear so I couldn't hear anything else. Then he went, "Well, I…" but Robert Hyde had already hung up. Dad clicked his phone shut, and I thought he was fired but instead he shouted, "I got the job! I'm going to be a DJ!"

He picked me up and whirled me round then,

and everyone was cheering. He told me *chutzpah* is having the bravery to take risks even if it means things might get difficult. I told him me and Jules and Tilda already call that something else, which is being a Stand-up Babe.

Then Dad said he wanted to celebrate by singing all 6 verses of "American Pie" on the karaoke machine. Because it was his special moment, even Mum had to be polite and listen to the awful racket. Luckily I didn't because I pretended to badly need the loo, and then I slipped off to the kitchen to get a drink.

Sangria was definitely not allowable for the very-nearly-teenagers and all the Coke had run out, so the choice was between a coffee and a Panda Pop like in the park café with Nan. *spooky or what?!* It made me have that wondering again, about which Lucy I am. Like, am I the grown-up cool one or the not-so-grown-up-no-make-up-Nan-cuddling one?

Well, I was just about to choose which drink

to have when Tilda and Jules came and grabbed me to do a song together on the karaoke machine. We all linked arms and crowded round the one mike, and Dad did a big DJ intro for us, calling us The BFF like we are still a band. And then we did "Girls Just Wanna Have Fun", and we totally had FUN doing it. *Spooky or what?!*

Eeeeekkkkk!, my pages have all gone *ka-poof!* The Easter holidays start in one week so I'll buy a new journal then and write loads more girly goss! But for now it's Goodbye From Me and Goodbye From, erm, Me again!

Goodbye!!!

Lucy,

XX.

# Lucy Jessica Hartley's Lurve Quiz

*Is he The One, a crush, or just a friend?*
*Find out with my fab quiz!!!*

1. *You spot your boy outside the science lab.*
*Do you:*
A) Go bright red, but manage to string a few
   words together. It would be easier if your
   mates stopped nudging each other and
   giggling, though!
B) Stop to chat about loads of different stuff,
   except Qs, bras and spells, of course!
   Those things are strictly for the girls!
C) Have a giant attack of *Cringitis* and end
   up just going *urgle-urgle* even though you
   planned loads of cool things to say the
   night before!

2. *You secretly...*
A) Imagine him asking you to Rollerworld,
   but only as part of a group.
B) Think about pinching his prized *Buffy* DVDs
   for a sleepover with your BFF.
C) Practise signing your name with his surname
   added on the end.

3. Which of these pictures most remind you of him?

A)  B)  C)

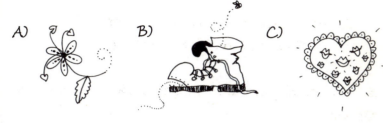

4. Your lad's eyes are:
A) Erm, blue, I think, or maybe brown?
B) Useful for seeing with… That's about it.
C) Stunningly gorgeous, like the sunset melting into a tropical sea.

*Mostly As: Crushtastic!* This boy could be the one for you, or you might have forgotten all about him by next week. Either way, enjoy it, you've got the balance just right!

*Mostly Bs: Mate not Date!* This boy is destined to stay in the Friendship Zone, but when you do meet someone you really fancy, he'll be there to big you up to your crush and teach you how to talk footie!

*Mostly Cs: Crazy in Love!* You're mad for this lad, but beware – love is blind! Sure, ask him out, but don't forget to make time for your **BFF** too.

# Totally Secret Info about Kelly McKain

**Lives:** In a small flat in Chiswick, West London, with a fridge full of chocolate.

**Life's ambition:** To be a showgirl in Paris 100 years ago. *(Erm, not really possible that one! – Ed.)* Okay, then, to be a writer – so I am actually doing it – yay! And also, to go on a flying trapeze.

**Star sign:** Capricorn (we're meant to be practical).

**Fave colour:** Purple.

**Fave animal:** Monkey.

**Ideal pet:** A purple monkey.

**Onstage embarrassment:** Performing a number from *Cats* in our dance school show. The black lycra catsuits were cool – the big fluffy tails were not! (Sorry, Miss Yvonne!)

**Fave hobbies:** Hanging out with my BFF and gorge boyf, watching *Friends*, going to yoga and dance classes, and playing my guitar as badly as Lucy's dad!

 **Find out more about Kelly at**
**www.kellymckain.co.uk**

## Have you read all of Lucy's hilarious journals?

# Makeover Magic

Lucy tries her makeover magic on the shy new girl at school.

*ISBN 9780746066898*

# Fantasy Fashion

Can Lucy design a fab enough outfit to win a fashion comp?

*ISBN 9780746066904*

# Star Struck

Lucy's in an actual film! Can she get her cool designs noticed?

*ISBN 9780746070611*

# Picture Perfect

Will crossed wires ruin Lucy's plans for a surprise birthday party?

*ISBN 9780746070628*

# Style School

Lucy's started a secret Style School club, but will Mr. Cain find out?

*ISBN 9780746070635*

# Summer Stars

The girls enter a beach party dance comp together on their hols!

*ISBN 9780746080177*

# Catwalk Crazy

Can Lucy uncover the secret saboteur of her charity fashion show?

*ISBN 9780746080184*

# Planet Fashion

Will Lucy's eco-makeover on Tilda's bedroom be on TV?

*ISBN 9780746080191*

# Best Friends Forever

It's the girls' ultra-glam prom...but who will Lucy go with?

*ISBN 9780746080207*

For Sue Chroston, who gave me
my first commission.

With special thanks to rock and roll goddess Jill
Marshall, for all the Earl Grey, guitar nights, laughs and
huge support when all this was just a twinkle in
a budding author's eye. Mwah!

First published in the UK in 2005 by Usborne Publishing Ltd., Usborne House, 83-85 Saffron Hill, London EC1N 8RT, England. www.usborne.com

Copyright © Kelly McKain, 2005. All rights reserved.

The right of Kelly McKain to be identified as the author of this work has been asserted by her in accordance with the Copyright, Designs and Patents Act, 1988.

Illustrations by Vici Leyhane.

The name Usborne and the devices ♀🎈 are Trade Marks of Usborne Publishing Ltd.

A CIP catalogue record for this book is available from the British Library.

 FMAMJJASOND/10  96687
ISBN 9780746066911
Printed in Yeovil, Somerset, UK.